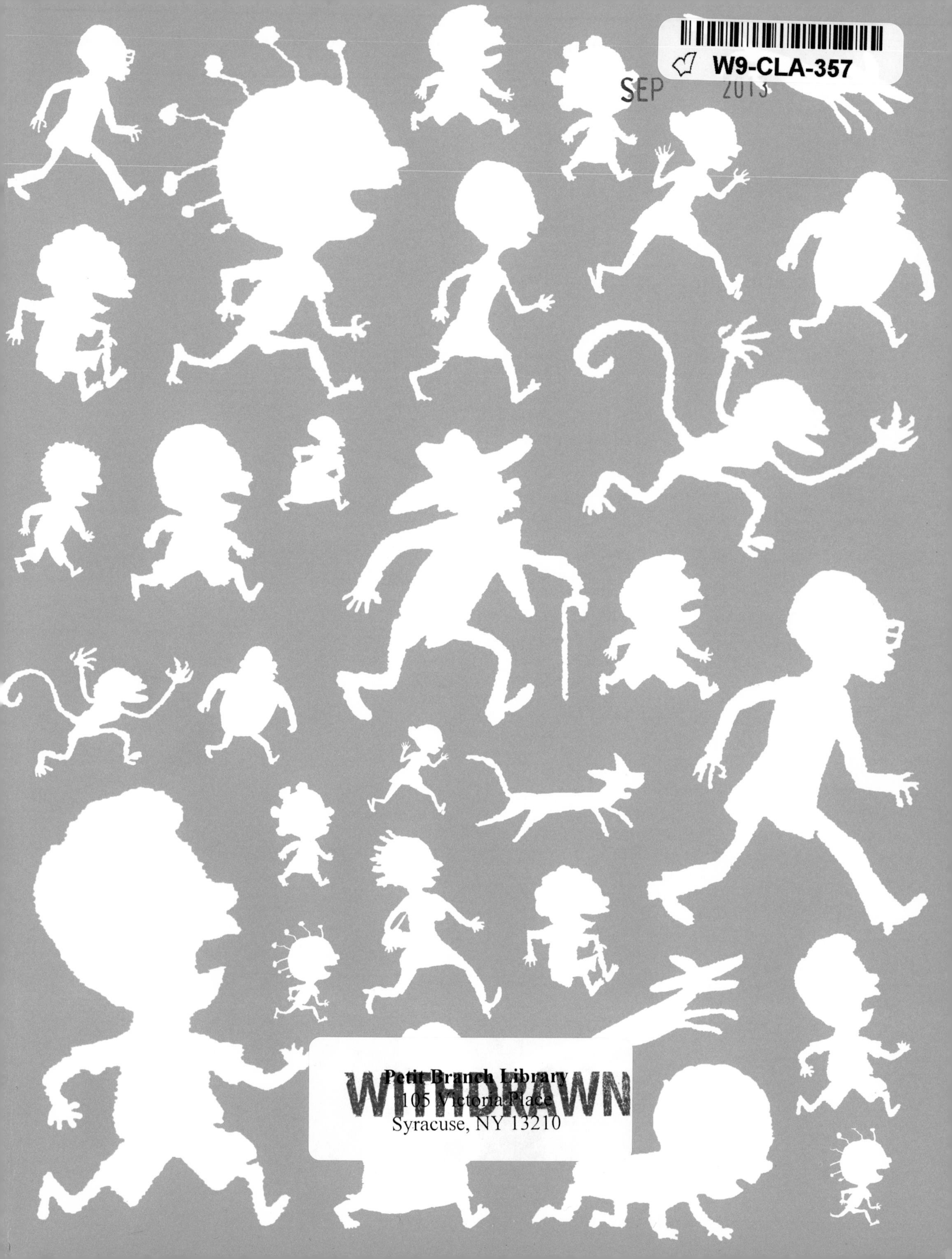

Marguerite ABOUET

Mathieu SAPIN

Akissi

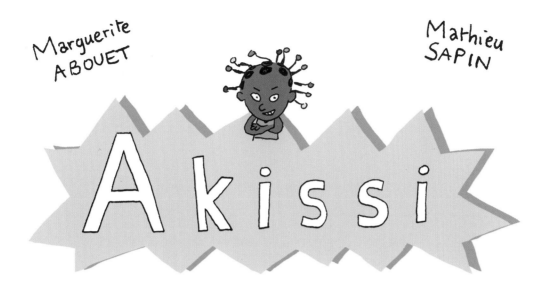

CAT INVASION

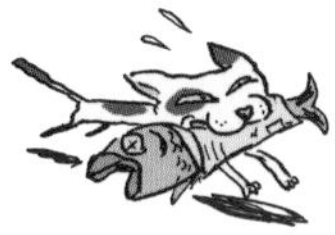

FLYING EYE BOOKS

To Marie Badomin, with all my love
M. A.

Thank you, Yvette for the precious Ivorian DVDs
M. S.

Inspired by the visual world
of Clément Oubrerie

Colouring by Clémence

Akissi, Cat Invasion (Akissi, Attaque de Chats) by Marguerite Abouet and Mathieu Sapin.
All artwork and characters within are © 2010 Gallimard Jeunesse.
This is a first English edition.
Translated from French by J. Taboy. This translation is © 2013 Flying Eye Books.
Edited by A. Spiro, sub-editing by S. G. Kennedy.
Additional cover design by A. Spiro. Typesetting by Mina Bach.
Published by arrangement with Gallimard Jeunesse.

Published by Flying Eye Books, an imprint of Nobrow Ltd.
62 Great Eastern Street, London, EC2A 3QR.

ISBN: 978-1-909263-01-7
Order from www.flyingeyebooks.com

FSC
www.fsc.org
MIX
Paper from
responsible sources
FSC® C101807

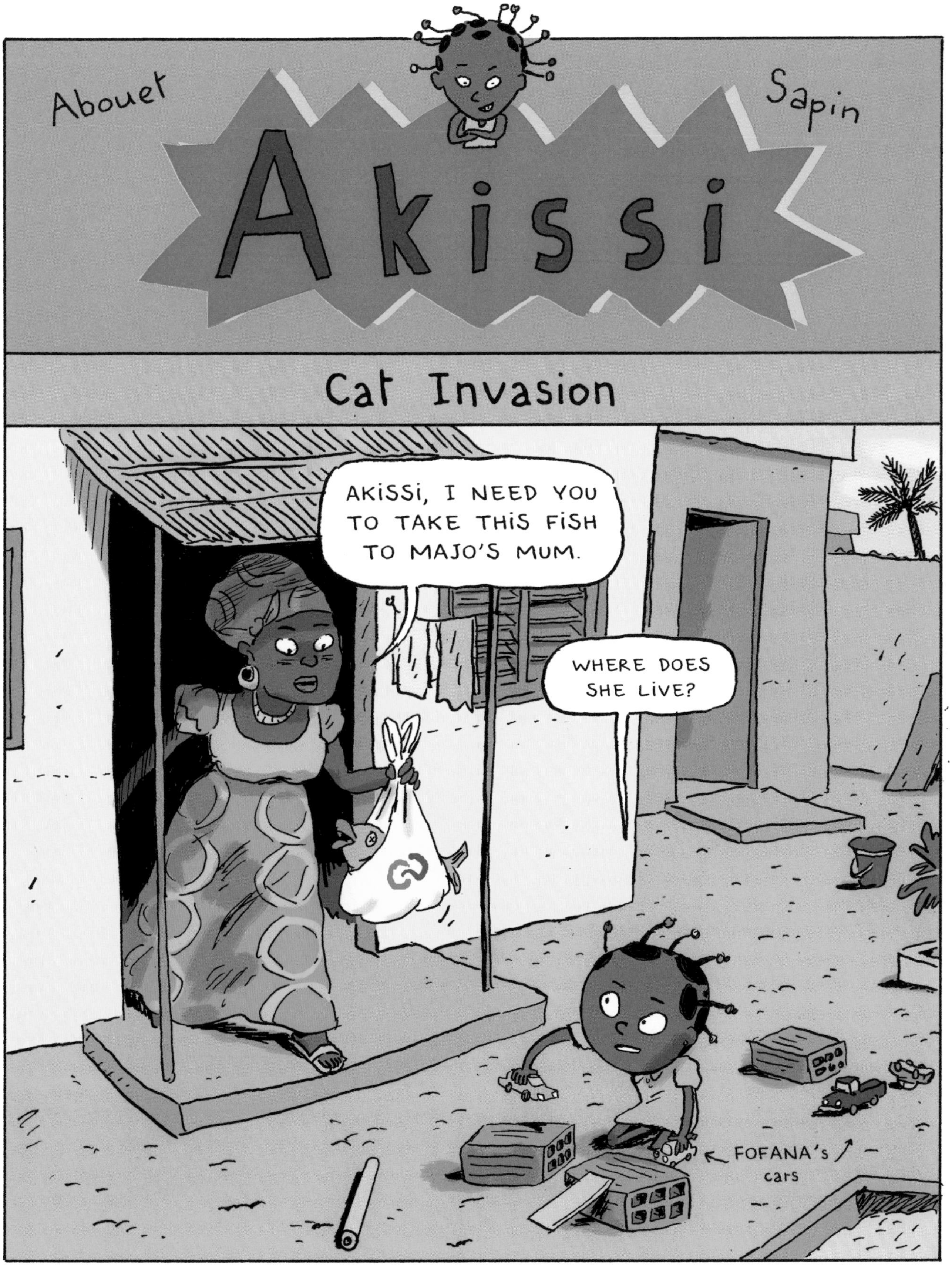
Abouet
Sapin
Akissi
Cat Invasion
AKiSSi, I NEED YOU TO TAKE THiS FiSH TO MAJO'S MUM.
WHERE DOES SHE LiVE?
FOFANA's cars

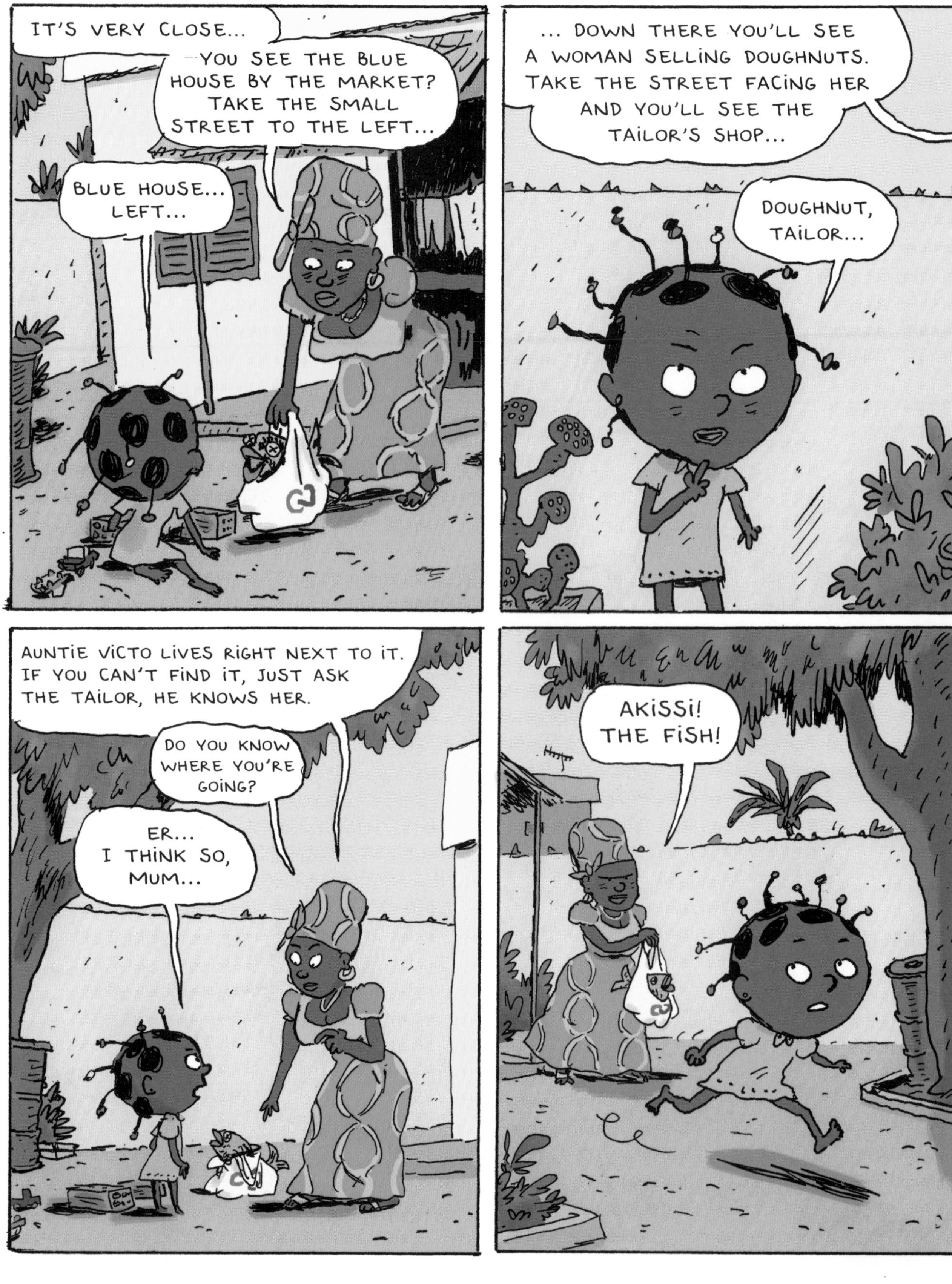
IT'S VERY CLOSE...
YOU SEE THE BLUE HOUSE BY THE MARKET? TAKE THE SMALL STREET TO THE LEFT...
BLUE HOUSE... LEFT...
... DOWN THERE YOU'LL SEE A WOMAN SELLING DOUGHNUTS. TAKE THE STREET FACING HER AND YOU'LL SEE THE TAILOR'S SHOP...
DOUGHNUT, TAILOR...
AUNTIE VICTO LIVES RIGHT NEXT TO IT. IF YOU CAN'T FIND IT, JUST ASK THE TAILOR, HE KNOWS HER.
DO YOU KNOW WHERE YOU'RE GOING?
ER... I THINK SO, MUM...
AKISSI! THE FISH!

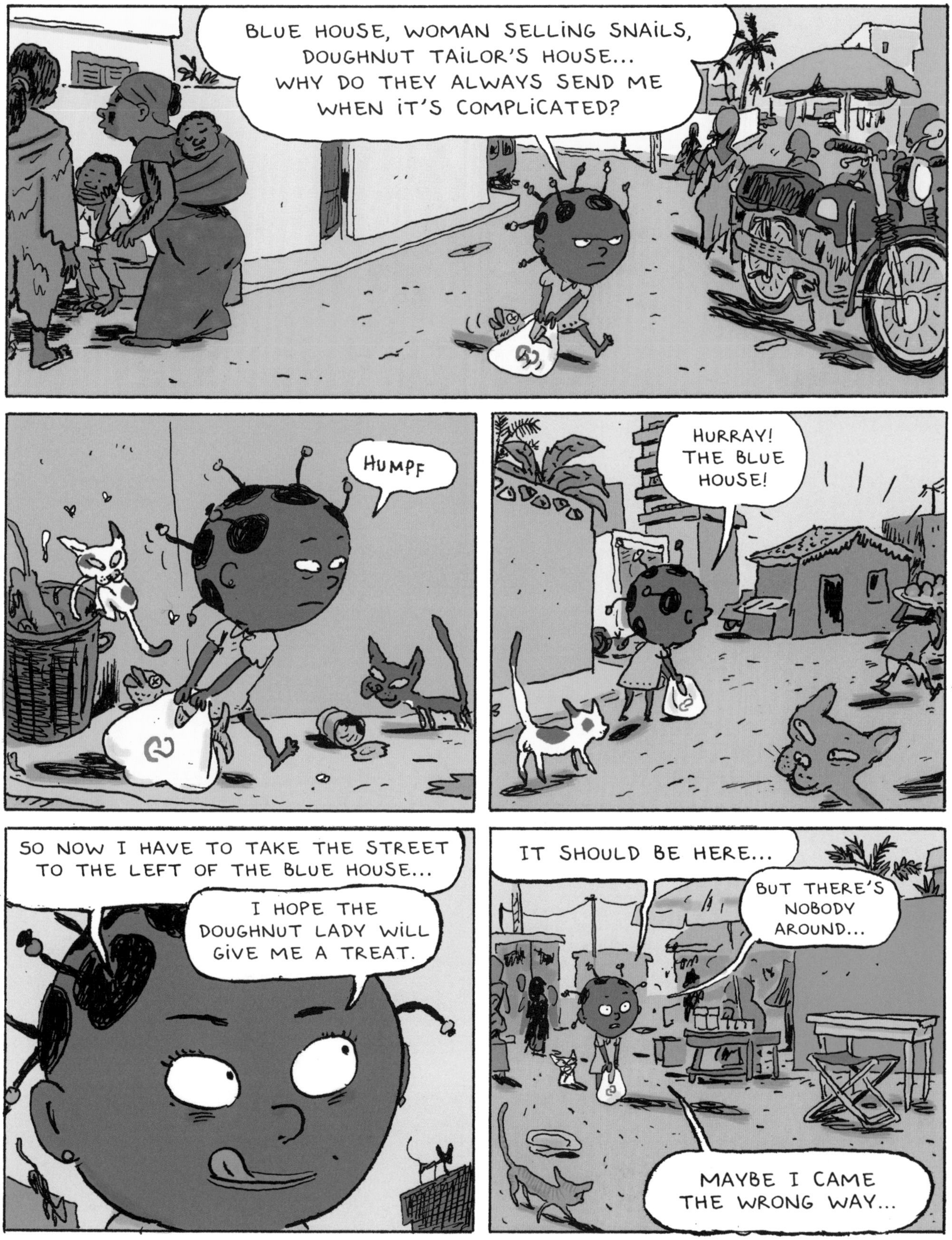
BLUE HOUSE, WOMAN SELLING SNAILS, DOUGHNUT TAILOR'S HOUSE... WHY DO THEY ALWAYS SEND ME WHEN IT'S COMPLICATED?
HUMPF
HURRAY! THE BLUE HOUSE!
SO NOW I HAVE TO TAKE THE STREET TO THE LEFT OF THE BLUE HOUSE...
I HOPE THE DOUGHNUT LADY WILL GIVE ME A TREAT.
IT SHOULD BE HERE...
BUT THERE'S NOBODY AROUND...
MAYBE I CAME THE WRONG WAY...

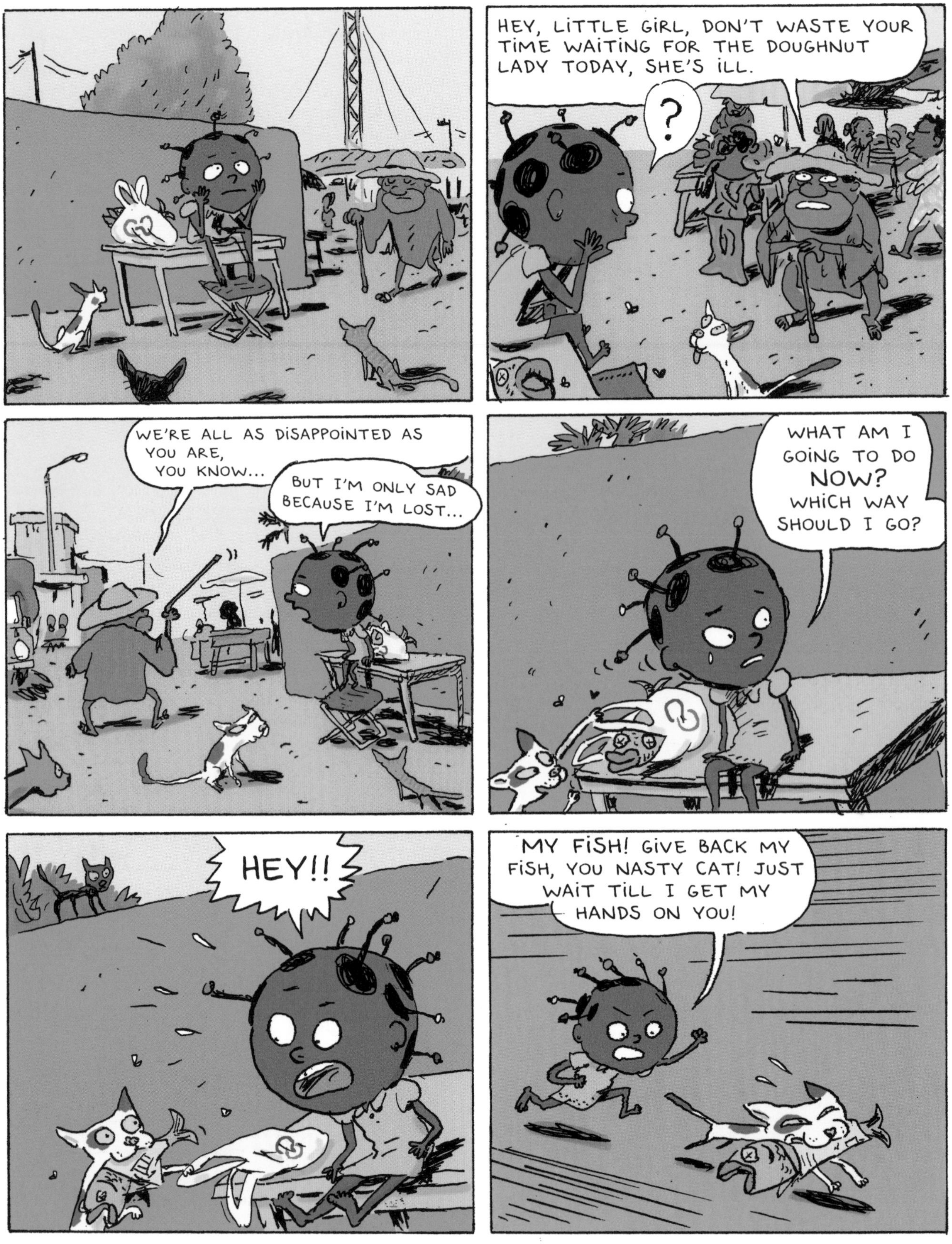
HEY, LITTLE GIRL, DON'T WASTE YOUR TIME WAITING FOR THE DOUGHNUT LADY TODAY, SHE'S ILL.
?
WE'RE ALL AS DISAPPOINTED AS YOU ARE, YOU KNOW...
BUT I'M ONLY SAD BECAUSE I'M LOST...
WHAT AM I GOING TO DO NOW? WHICH WAY SHOULD I GO?
HEY!!
MY FISH! GIVE BACK MY FISH, YOU NASTY CAT! JUST WAIT TILL I GET MY HANDS ON YOU!

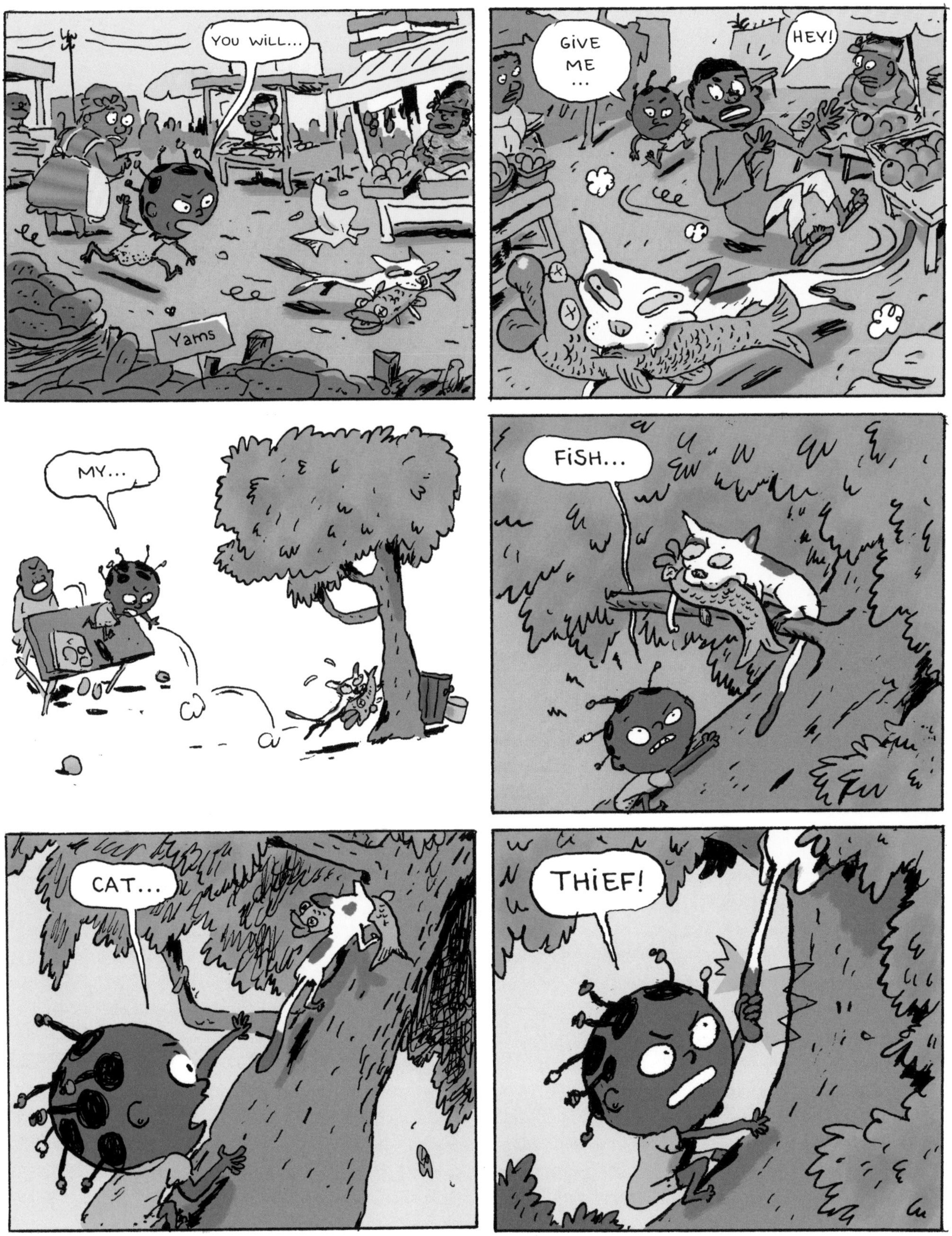

YOU WILL...
Yams
GIVE ME ...
HEY!
MY...
FISH...
CAT...
THIEF!

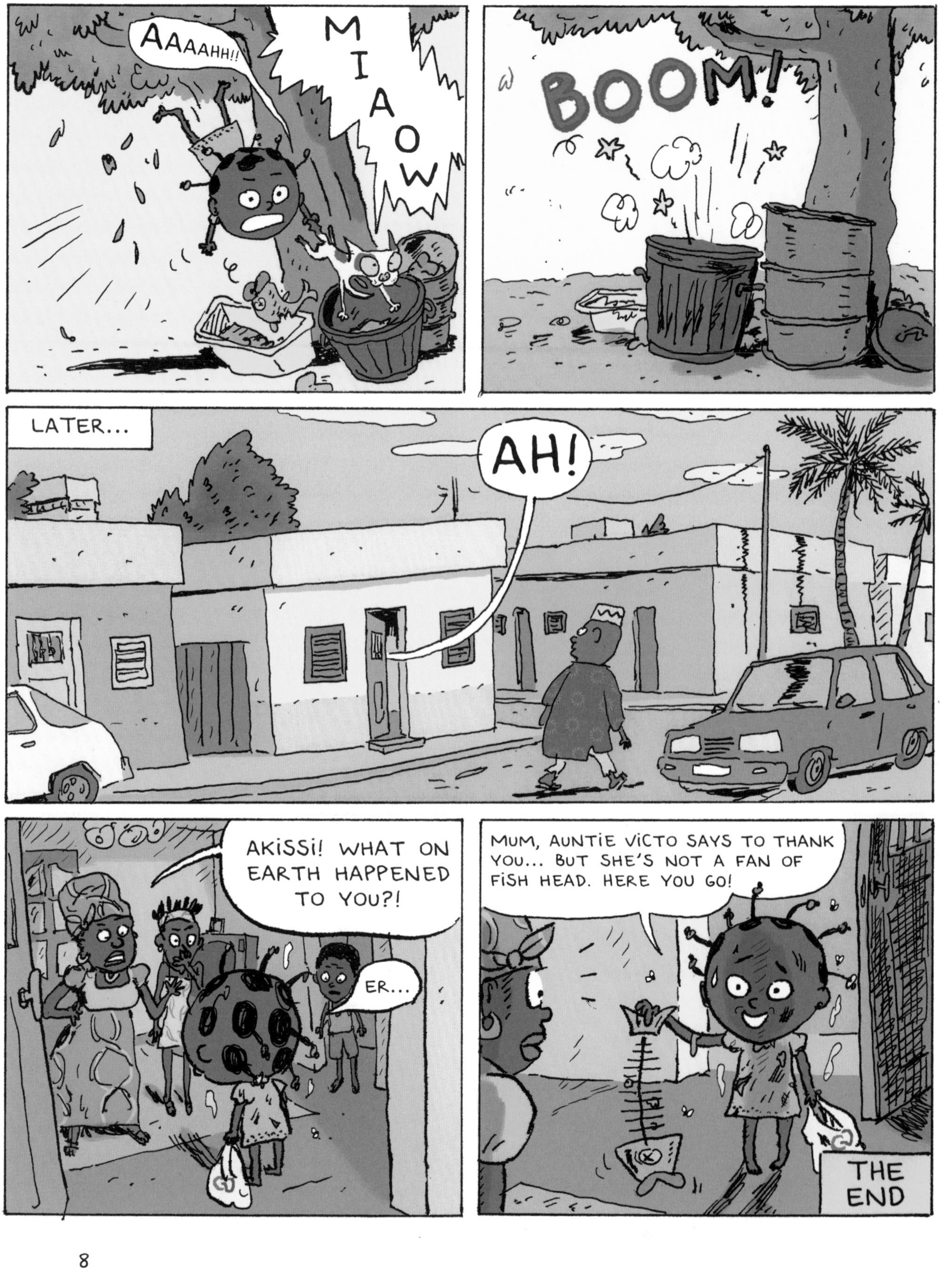
AAAAHH!!
MIAOW
BOOM!
LATER...
AH!
AKISSI! WHAT ON EARTH HAPPENED TO YOU?!
ER...
MUM, AUNTIE VICTO SAYS TO THANK YOU... BUT SHE'S NOT A FAN OF FISH HEAD. HERE YOU GO!
THE END

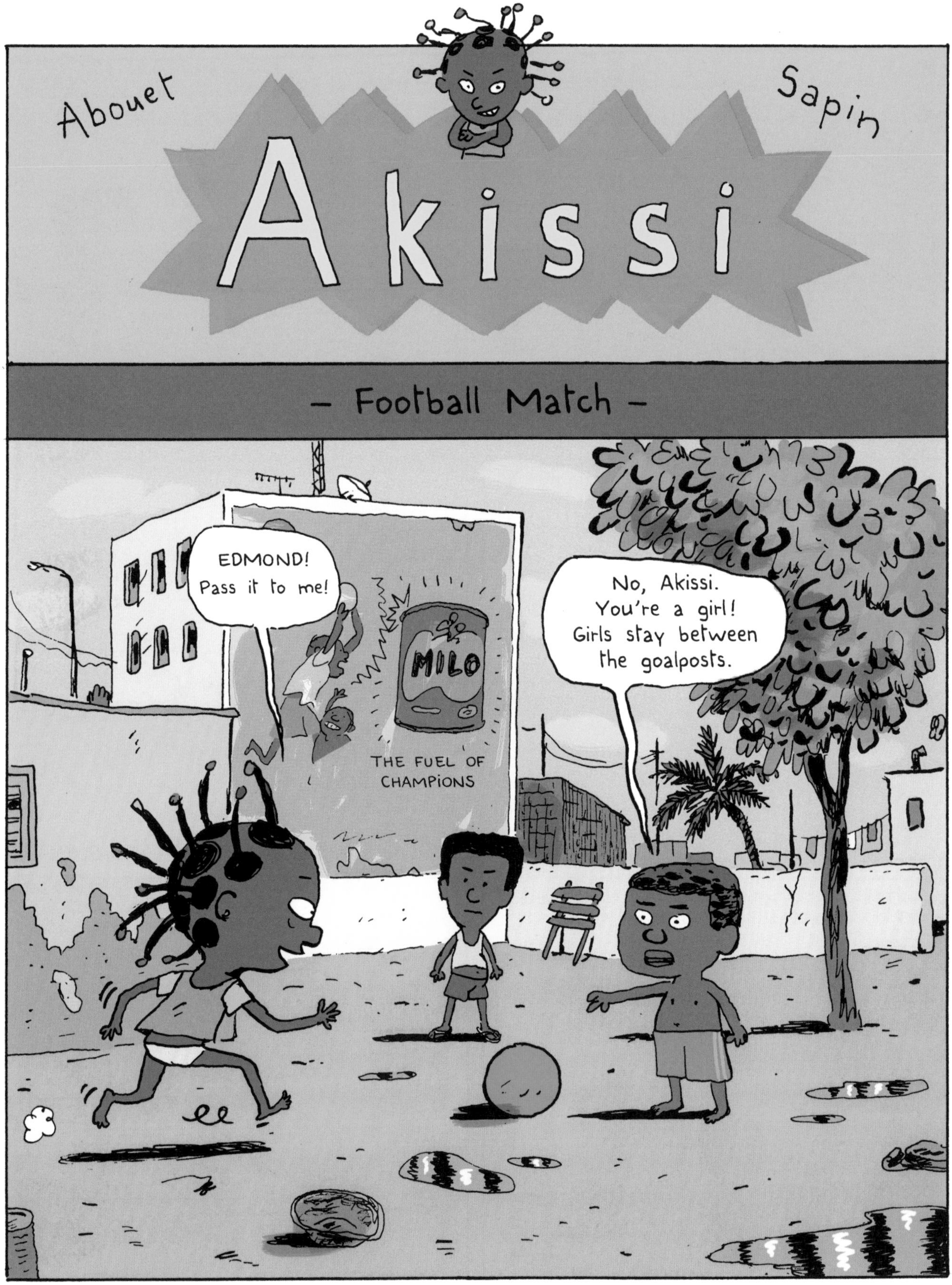
Abouet
Sapin
Akissi
- Football Match -
EDMOND! Pass it to me!
MILO
THE FUEL OF CHAMPIONS
No, Akissi. You're a girl! Girls stay between the goalposts.

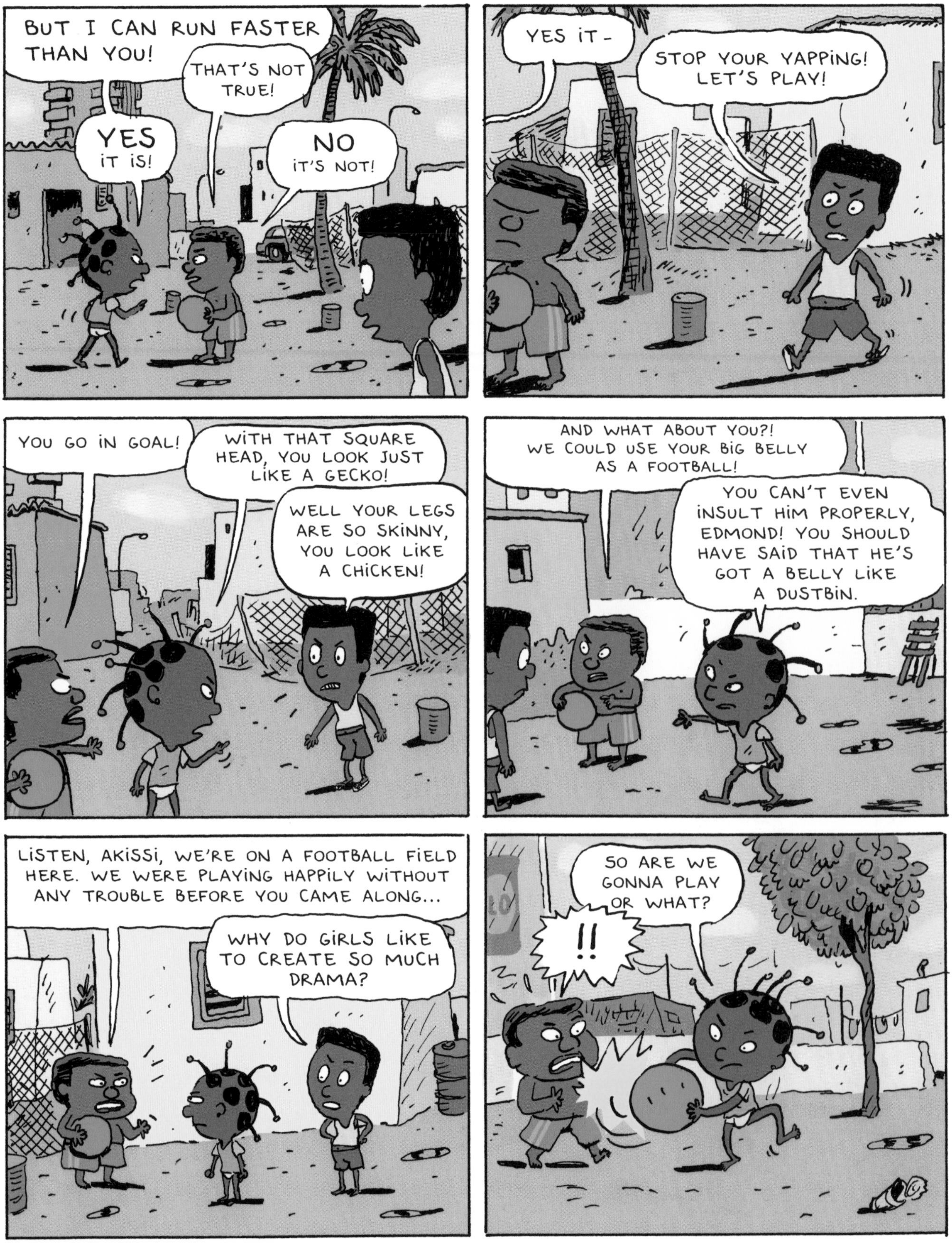
BUT I CAN RUN FASTER THAN YOU!
THAT'S NOT TRUE!
YES iT iS!
NO iT'S NOT!
YES iT -
STOP YOUR YAPPiNG! LET'S PLAY!
YOU GO iN GOAL!
WiTH THAT SQUARE HEAD, YOU LOOK JUST LiKE A GECKO!
WELL YOUR LEGS ARE SO SKiNNY, YOU LOOK LiKE A CHiCKEN!
AND WHAT ABOUT YOU?! WE COULD USE YOUR BiG BELLY AS A FOOTBALL!
YOU CAN'T EVEN iNSULT HiM PROPERLY, EDMOND! YOU SHOULD HAVE SAiD THAT HE'S GOT A BELLY LiKE A DUSTBiN.
LiSTEN, AKiSSi, WE'RE ON A FOOTBALL FiELD HERE. WE WERE PLAYiNG HAPPiLY WiTHOUT ANY TROUBLE BEFORE YOU CAME ALONG...
WHY DO GiRLS LiKE TO CREATE SO MUCH DRAMA?
SO ARE WE GONNA PLAY OR WHAT?
!!

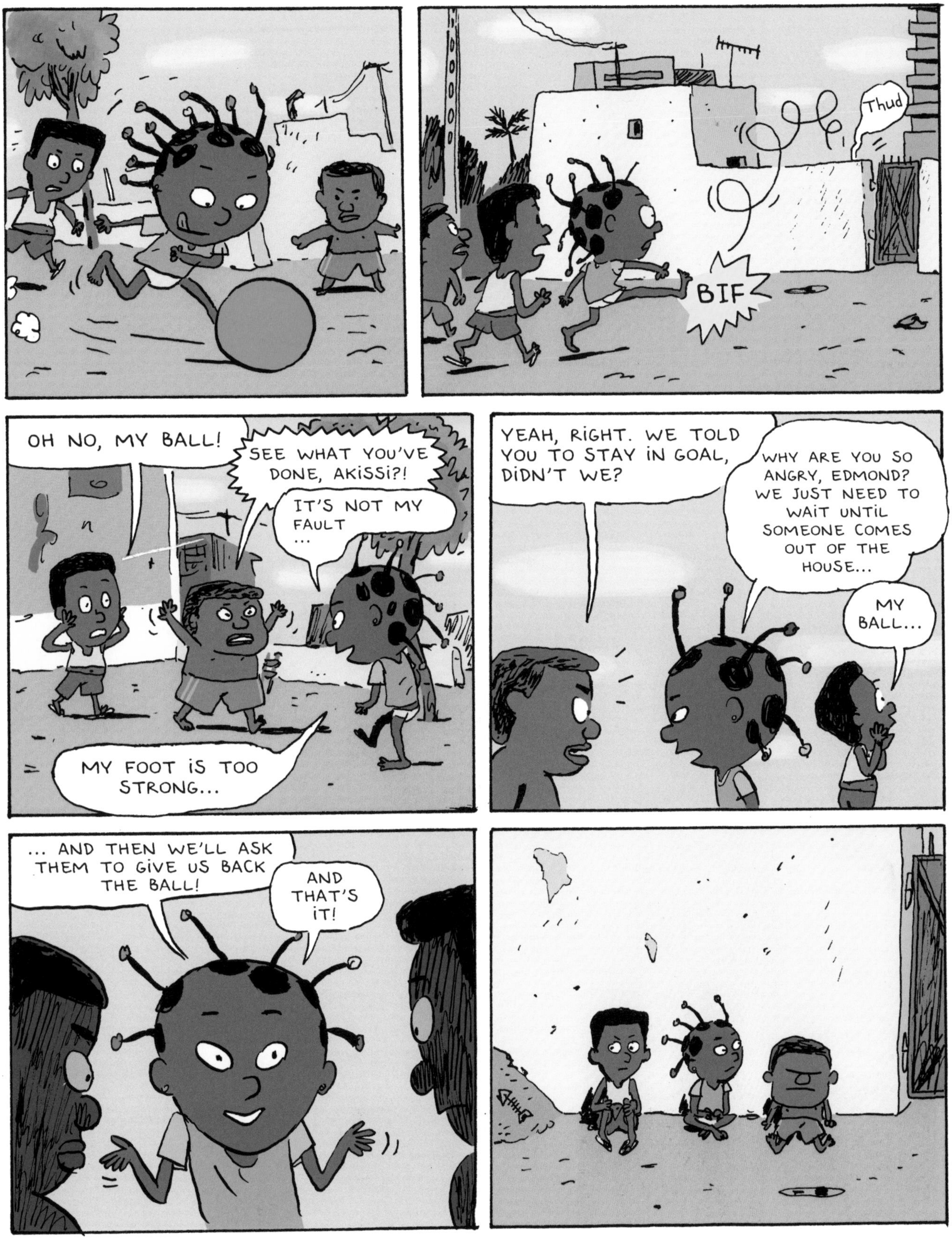
Thud
BIF
OH NO, MY BALL!
SEE WHAT YOU'VE DONE, AKiSSi?!
IT'S NOT MY FAULT ...
MY FOOT iS TOO STRONG...
YEAH, RiGHT. WE TOLD YOU TO STAY iN GOAL, DiDN'T WE?
WHY ARE YOU SO ANGRY, EDMOND? WE JUST NEED TO WAiT UNTiL SOMEONE COMES OUT OF THE HOUSE...
MY BALL...
... AND THEN WE'LL ASK THEM TO GiVE US BACK THE BALL!
AND THAT'S iT!

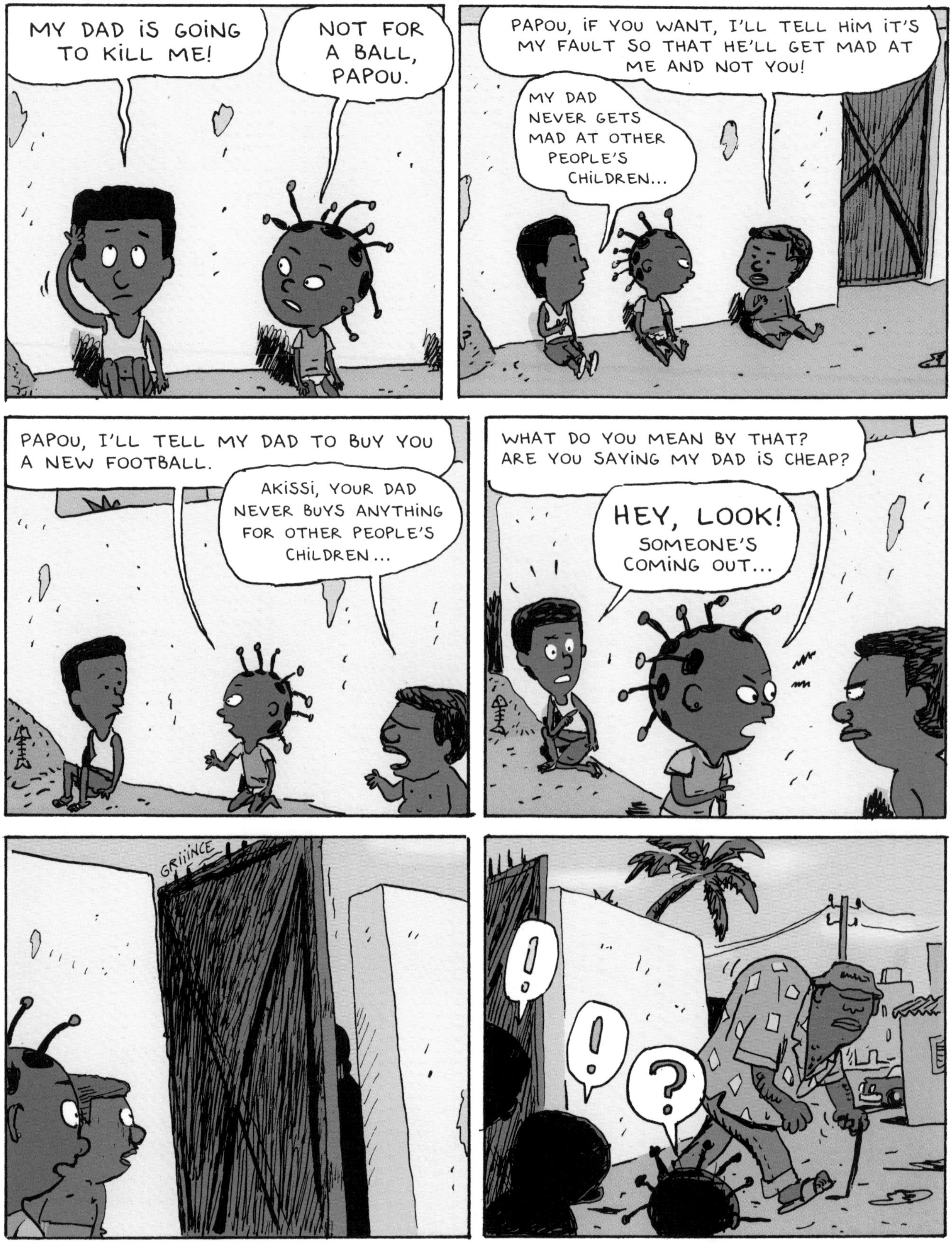
MY DAD IS GOING TO KILL ME!
NOT FOR A BALL, PAPOU.
PAPOU, IF YOU WANT, I'LL TELL HIM IT'S MY FAULT SO THAT HE'LL GET MAD AT ME AND NOT YOU!
MY DAD NEVER GETS MAD AT OTHER PEOPLE'S CHILDREN...
PAPOU, I'LL TELL MY DAD TO BUY YOU A NEW FOOTBALL.
AKISSI, YOUR DAD NEVER BUYS ANYTHING FOR OTHER PEOPLE'S CHILDREN...
WHAT DO YOU MEAN BY THAT? ARE YOU SAYING MY DAD IS CHEAP?
HEY, LOOK! SOMEONE'S COMING OUT...
GRIIINCE
!
!
?

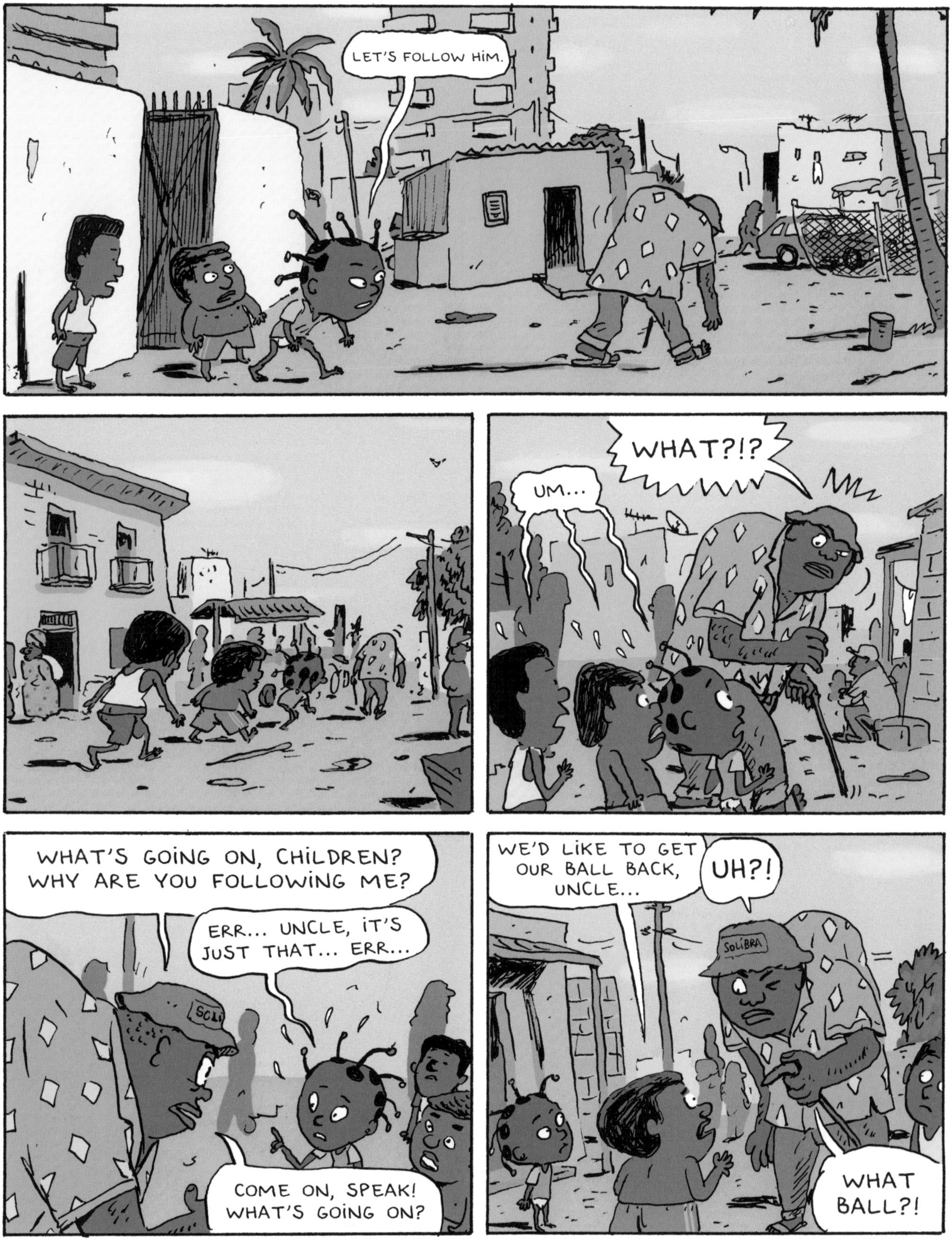
LET'S FOLLOW HIM.
UM...
WHAT?!?
WHAT'S GOING ON, CHILDREN? WHY ARE YOU FOLLOWING ME?
ERR... UNCLE, IT'S JUST THAT... ERR...
SOLI
COME ON, SPEAK! WHAT'S GOING ON?
WE'D LIKE TO GET OUR BALL BACK, UNCLE...
UH?!
SOLIBRA
WHAT BALL?!

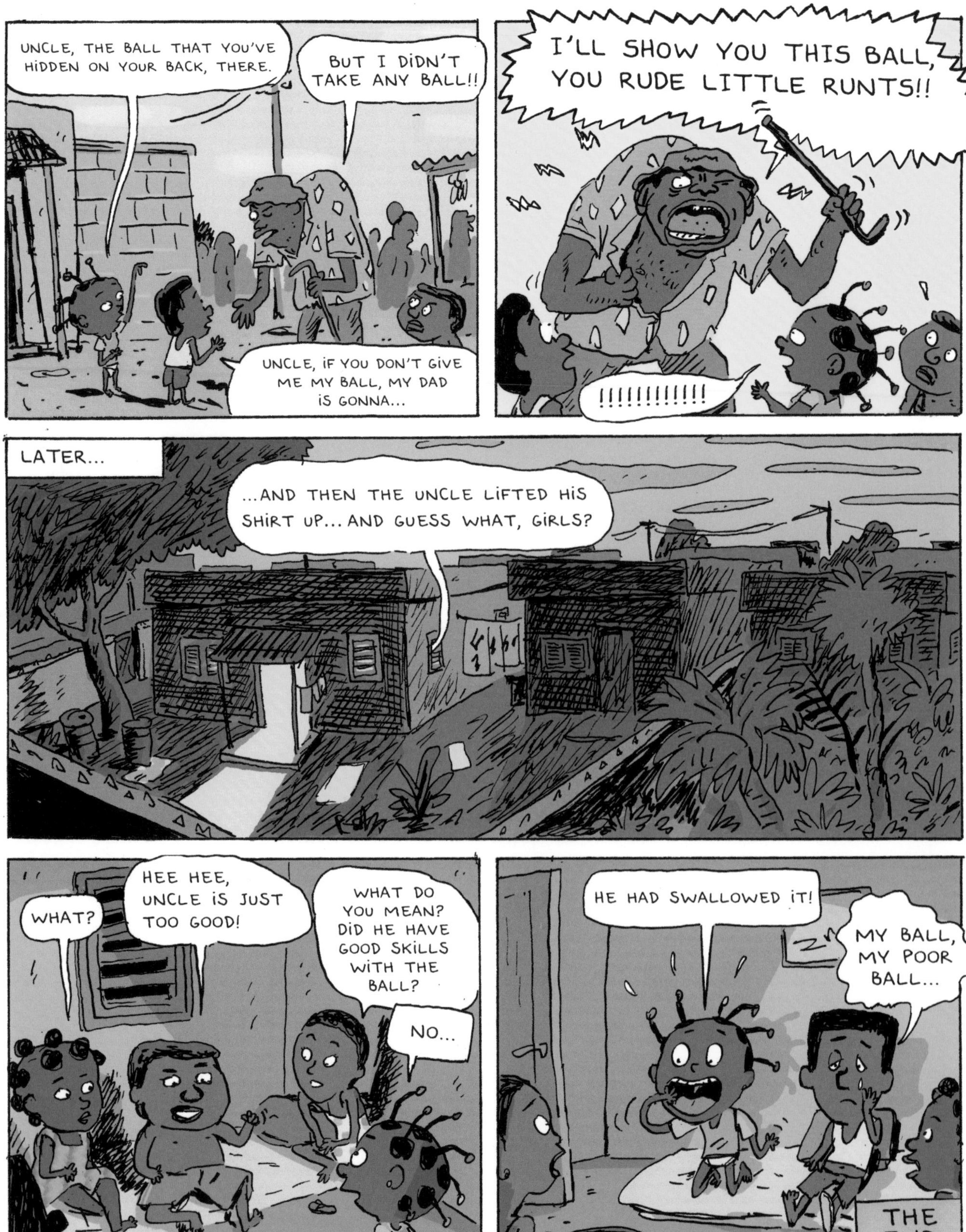
UNCLE, THE BALL THAT YOU'VE HIDDEN ON YOUR BACK, THERE.
BUT I DIDN'T TAKE ANY BALL!!
UNCLE, IF YOU DON'T GIVE ME MY BALL, MY DAD IS GONNA...
I'LL SHOW YOU THIS BALL, YOU RUDE LITTLE RUNTS!!
!!!!!!!!!!!!
LATER...
...AND THEN THE UNCLE LIFTED HIS SHIRT UP... AND GUESS WHAT, GIRLS?
WHAT?
HEE HEE, UNCLE IS JUST TOO GOOD!
WHAT DO YOU MEAN? DID HE HAVE GOOD SKILLS WITH THE BALL?
NO...
HE HAD SWALLOWED IT!
MY BALL, MY POOR BALL...
THE END

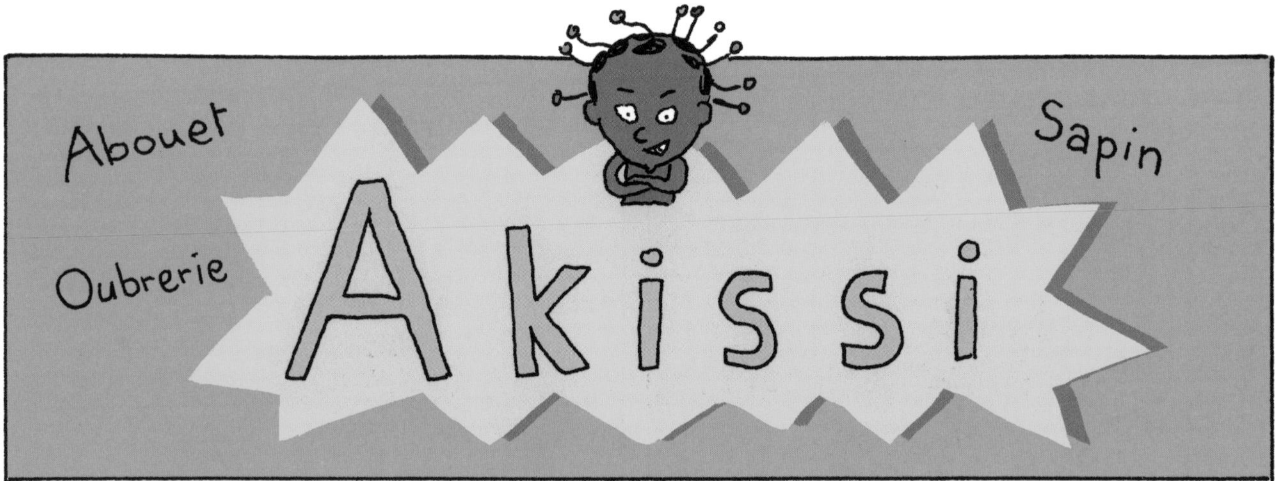
Abouet
Sapin
Oubrerie
Akissi

Good Mums

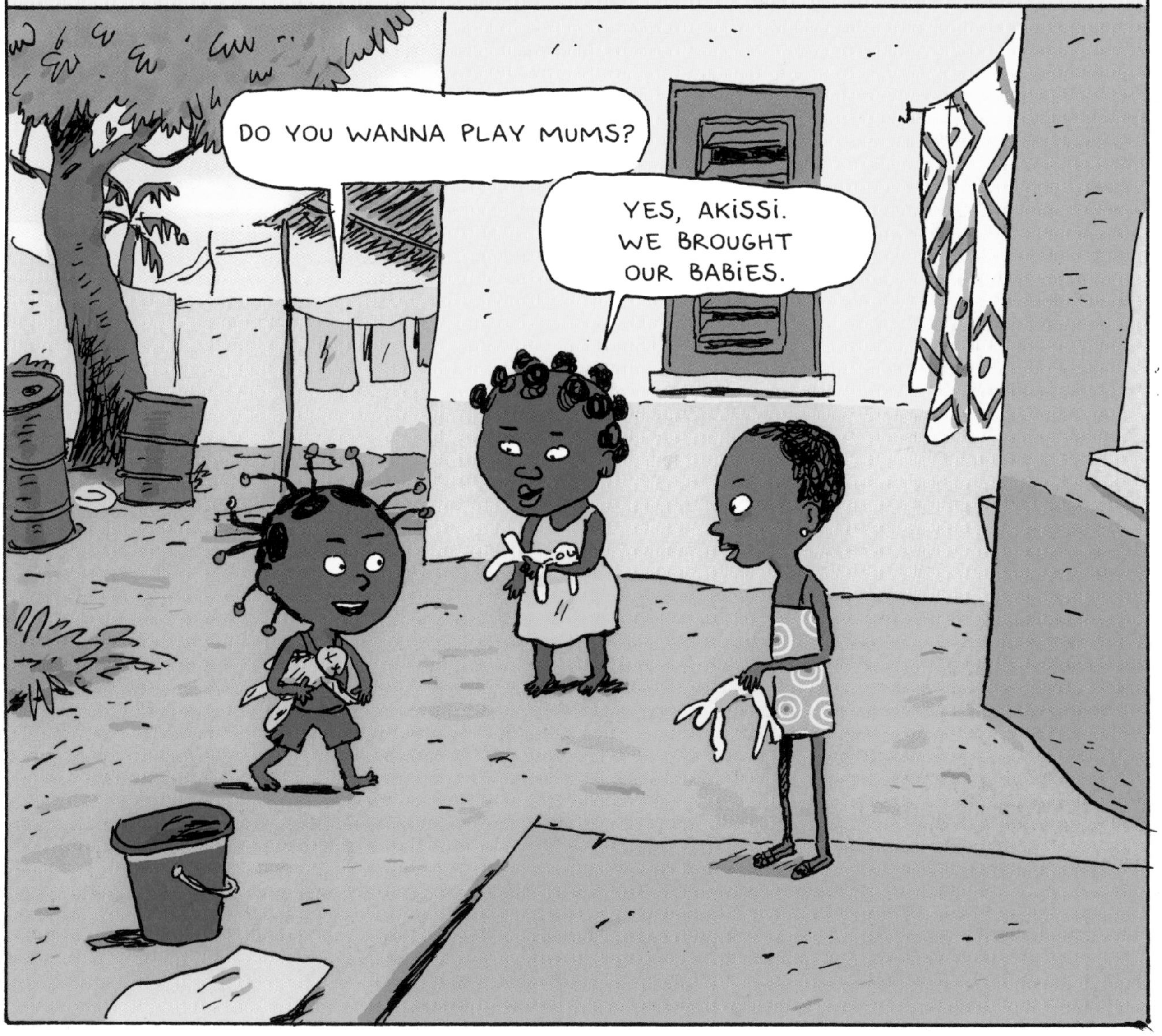
DO YOU WANNA PLAY MUMS?
YES, AKISSI. WE BROUGHT OUR BABIES.

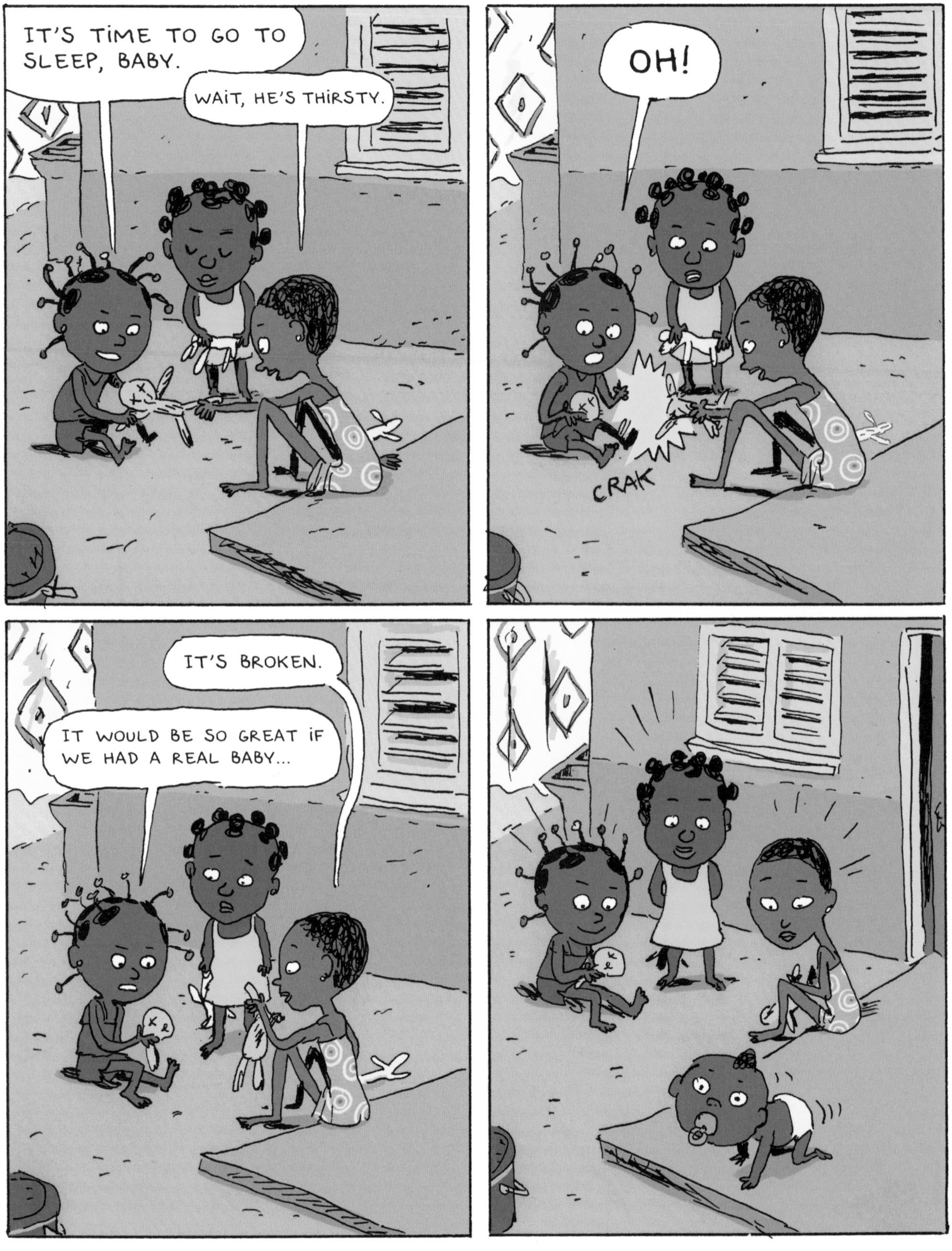
IT'S TIME TO GO TO SLEEP, BABY.
WAIT, HE'S THIRSTY.
OH!
CRAK
IT'S BROKEN.
IT WOULD BE SO GREAT IF WE HAD A REAL BABY...

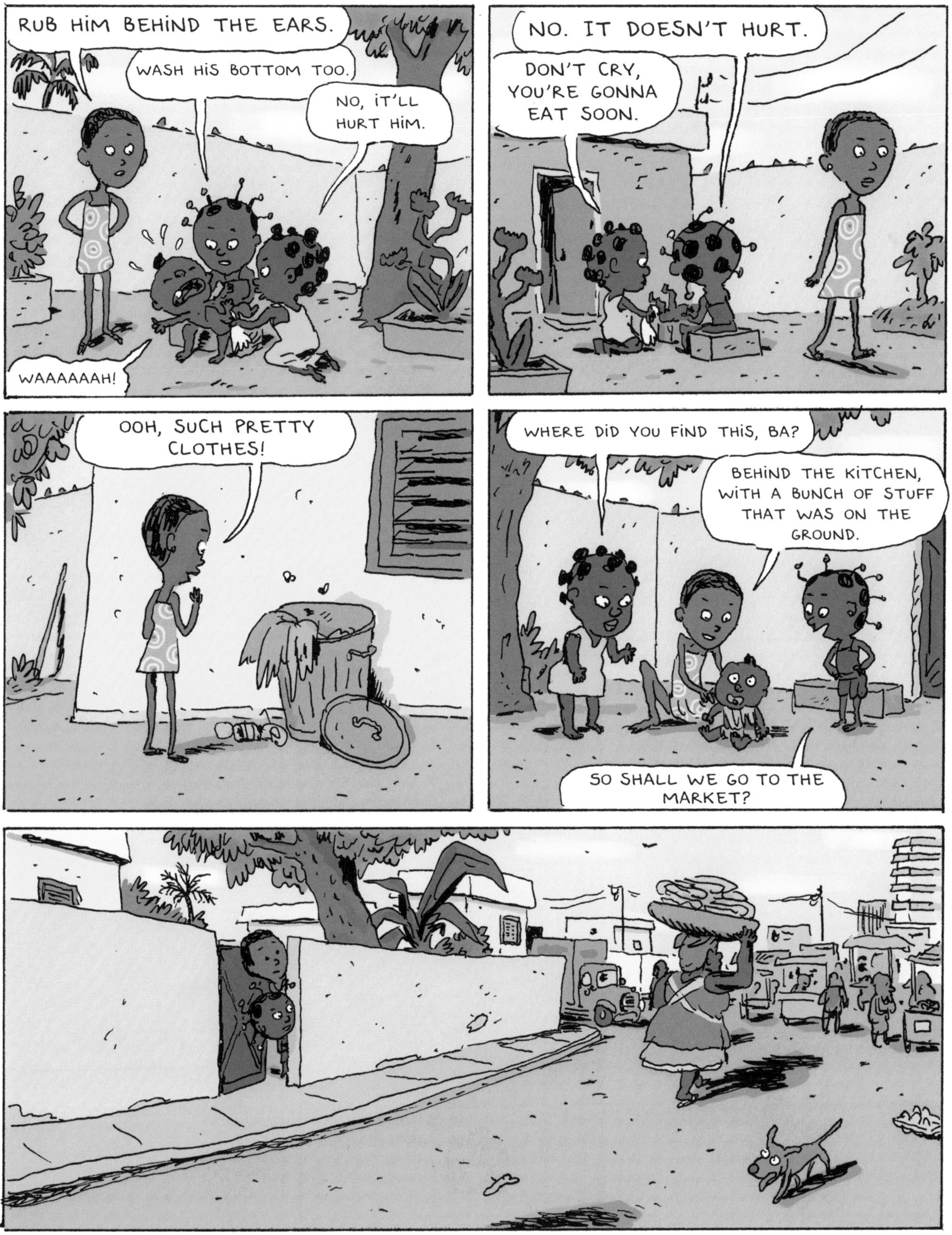
RUB HIM BEHIND THE EARS.
WASH HIS BOTTOM TOO.
NO, IT'LL HURT HIM.
WAAAAAAH!
NO. IT DOESN'T HURT.
DON'T CRY, YOU'RE GONNA EAT SOON.
OOH, SUCH PRETTY CLOTHES!
WHERE DID YOU FIND THIS, BA?
BEHIND THE KITCHEN, WITH A BUNCH OF STUFF THAT WAS ON THE GROUND.
SO SHALL WE GO TO THE MARKET?

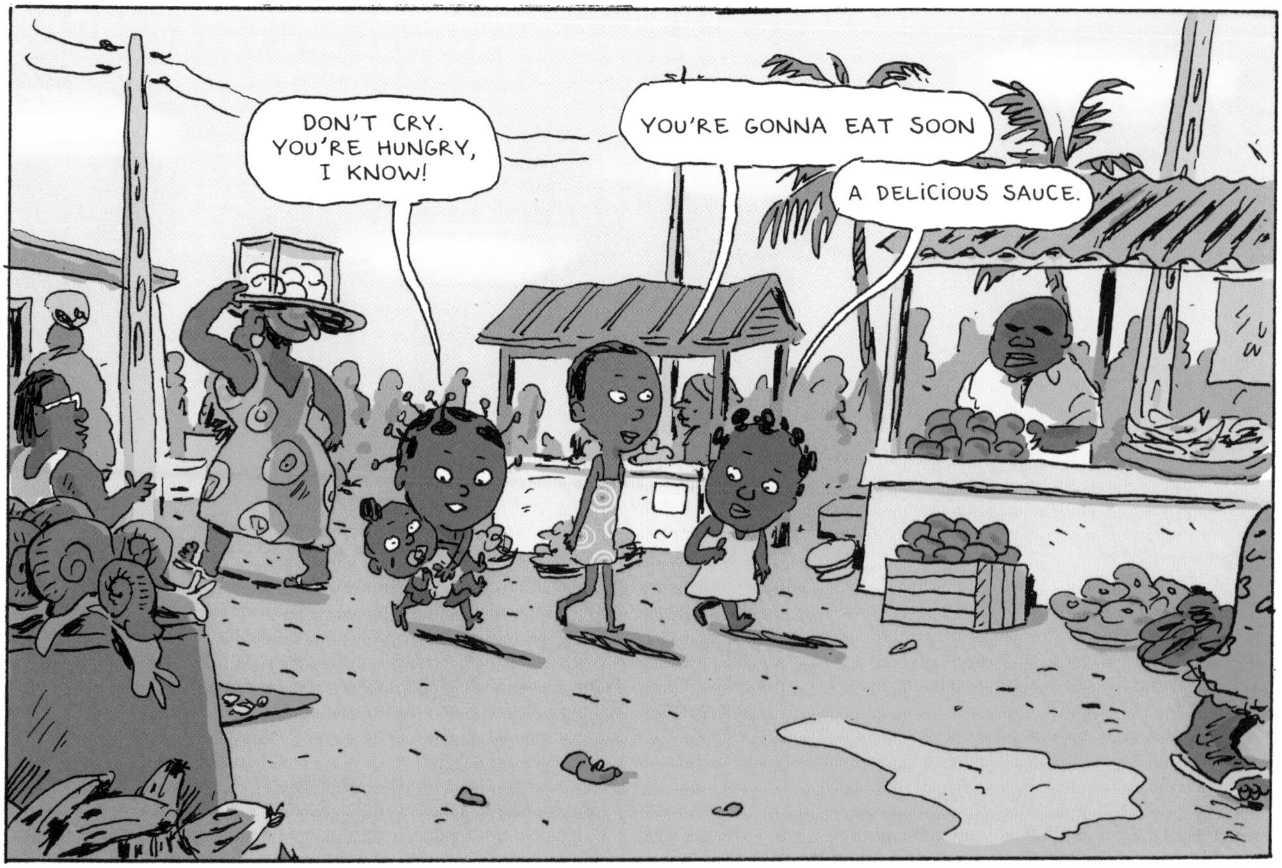
DON'T CRY. YOU'RE HUNGRY, I KNOW!
YOU'RE GONNA EAT SOON
A DELICIOUS SAUCE.

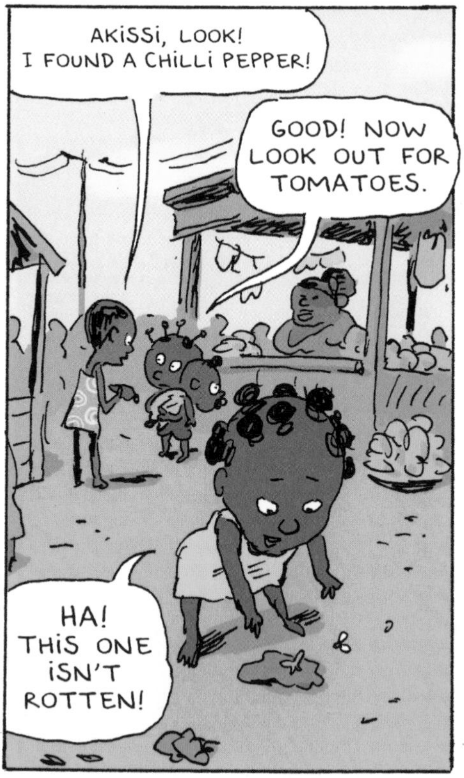
AKISSI, LOOK! I FOUND A CHILLI PEPPER!
GOOD! NOW LOOK OUT FOR TOMATOES.
HA! THIS ONE ISN'T ROTTEN!

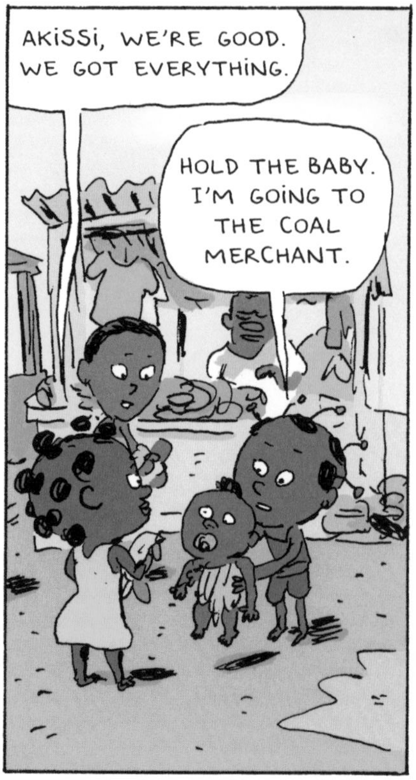
AKISSI, WE'RE GOOD. WE GOT EVERYTHING.
HOLD THE BABY. I'M GOING TO THE COAL MERCHANT.

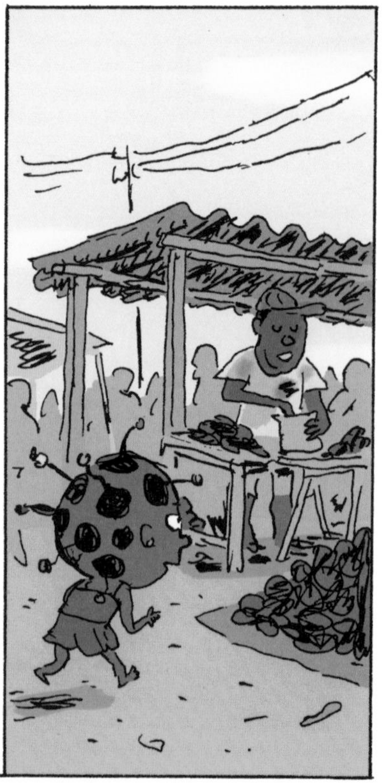

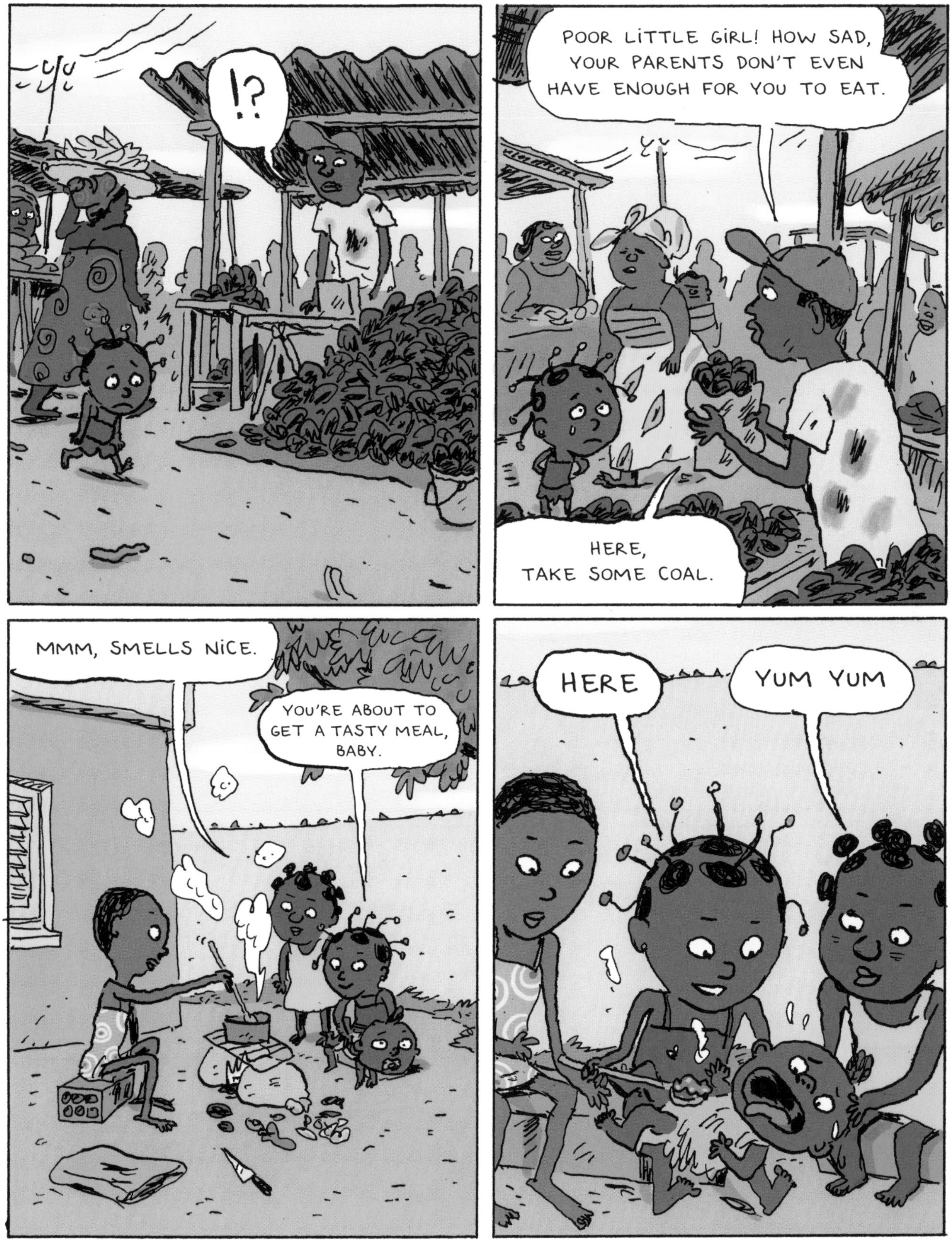
!?
POOR LITTLE GIRL! HOW SAD, YOUR PARENTS DON'T EVEN HAVE ENOUGH FOR YOU TO EAT.
HERE, TAKE SOME COAL.
MMM, SMELLS NICE.
YOU'RE ABOUT TO GET A TASTY MEAL, BABY.
HERE
YUM YUM

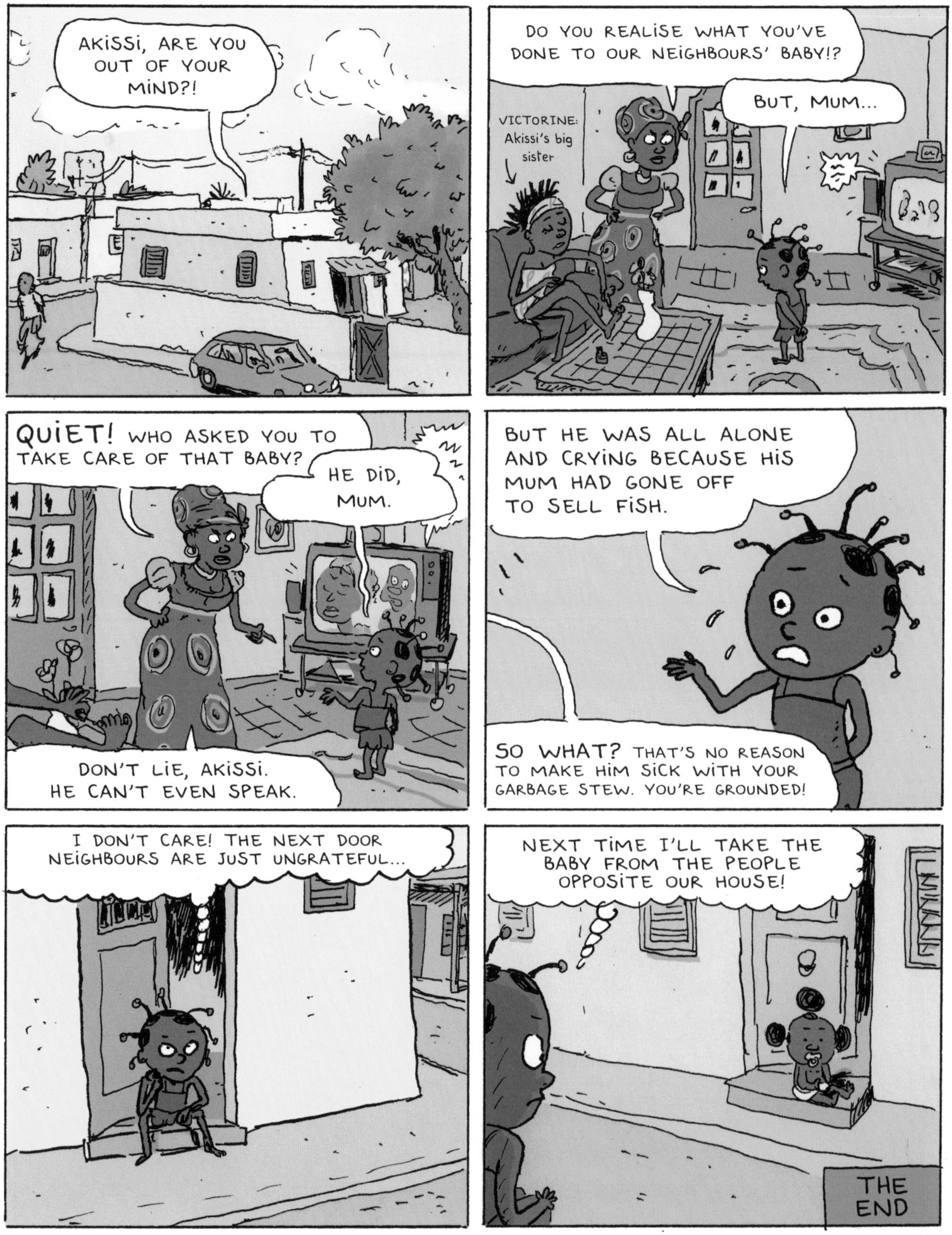
AKISSI, ARE YOU OUT OF YOUR MIND?!
DO YOU REALISE WHAT YOU'VE DONE TO OUR NEIGHBOURS' BABY!?
VICTORINE: Akissi's big sister
BUT, MUM...
QUIET! WHO ASKED YOU TO TAKE CARE OF THAT BABY?
HE DID, MUM.
DON'T LIE, AKISSI. HE CAN'T EVEN SPEAK.
BUT HE WAS ALL ALONE AND CRYING BECAUSE HIS MUM HAD GONE OFF TO SELL FISH.
SO WHAT? THAT'S NO REASON TO MAKE HIM SICK WITH YOUR GARBAGE STEW. YOU'RE GROUNDED!
I DON'T CARE! THE NEXT DOOR NEIGHBOURS ARE JUST UNGRATEFUL...
NEXT TIME I'LL TAKE THE BABY FROM THE PEOPLE OPPOSITE OUR HOUSE!
THE END

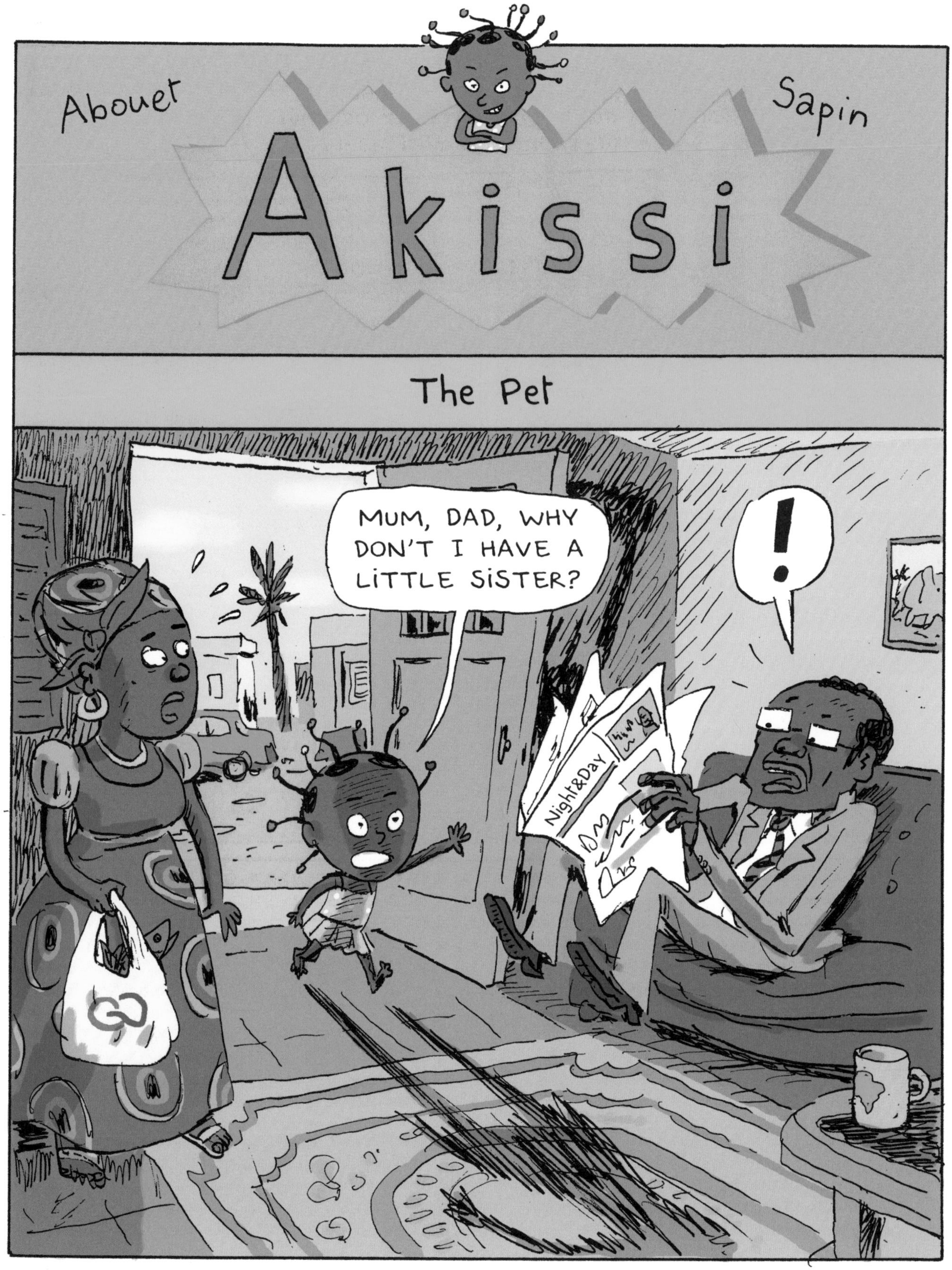
Abouet
Sapin
Akissi
The Pet
MUM, DAD, WHY DON'T I HAVE A LITTLE SISTER?
!
Night&Day

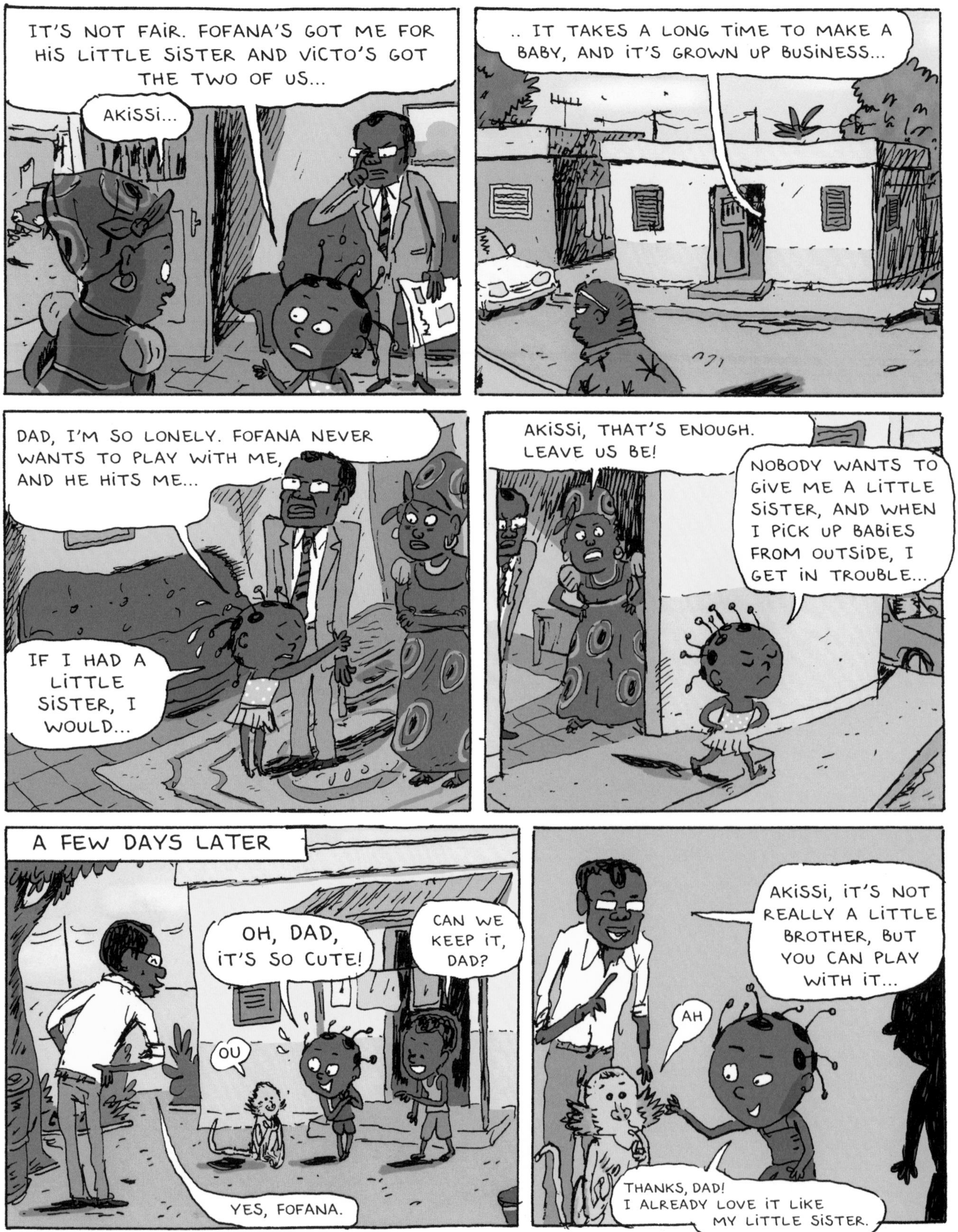
IT'S NOT FAIR. FOFANA'S GOT ME FOR HIS LITTLE SISTER AND VICTO'S GOT THE TWO OF US...
AKISSI...
.. IT TAKES A LONG TIME TO MAKE A BABY, AND IT'S GROWN UP BUSINESS...
DAD, I'M SO LONELY. FOFANA NEVER WANTS TO PLAY WITH ME, AND HE HITS ME...
IF I HAD A LITTLE SISTER, I WOULD...
AKISSI, THAT'S ENOUGH. LEAVE US BE!
NOBODY WANTS TO GIVE ME A LITTLE SISTER, AND WHEN I PICK UP BABIES FROM OUTSIDE, I GET IN TROUBLE...
A FEW DAYS LATER
OH, DAD, IT'S SO CUTE!
CAN WE KEEP IT, DAD?
OU
YES, FOFANA.
AKISSI, IT'S NOT REALLY A LITTLE BROTHER, BUT YOU CAN PLAY WITH IT...
AH
THANKS, DAD! I ALREADY LOVE IT LIKE MY LITTLE SISTER.

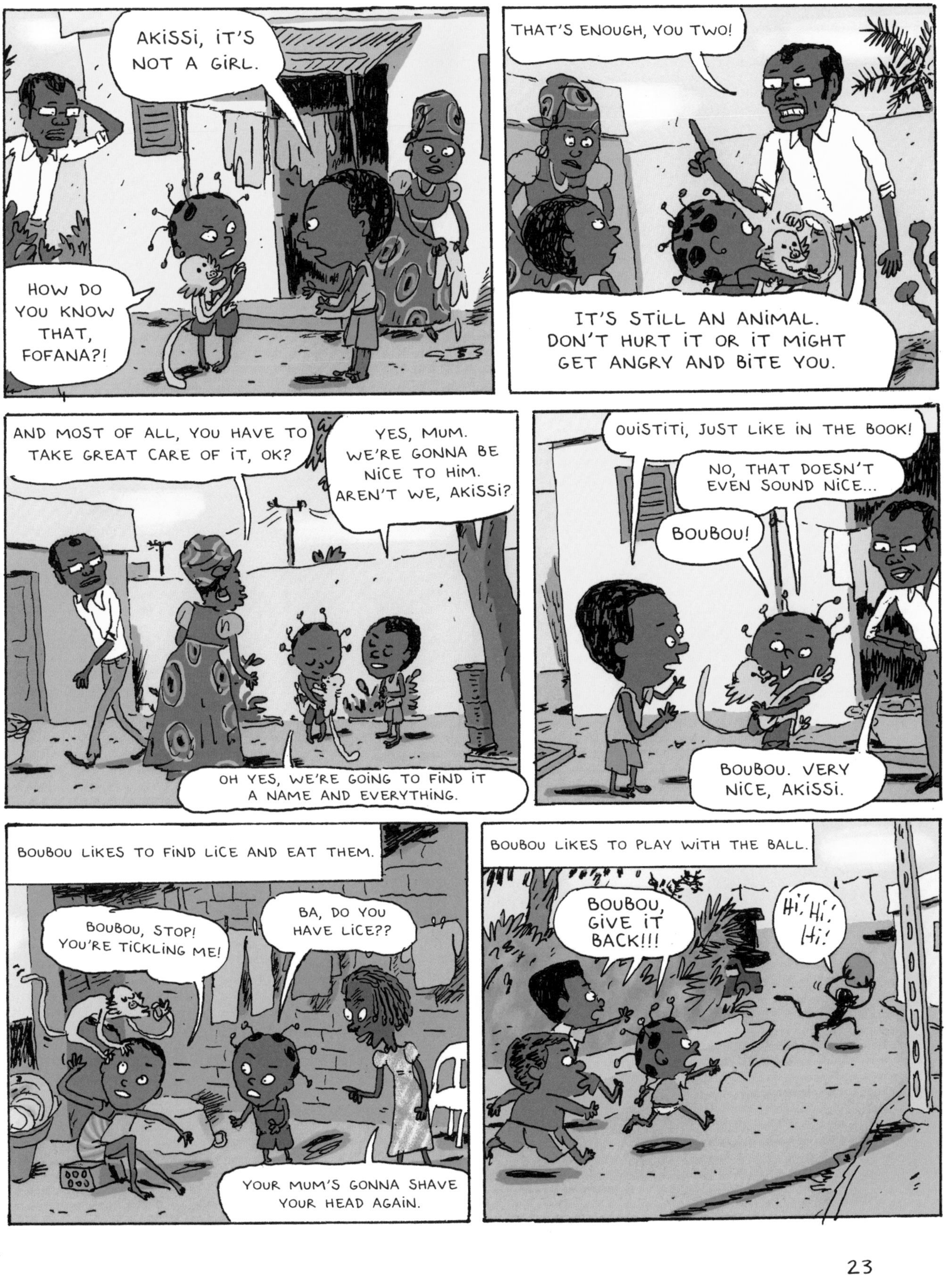
AKiSSi, iT'S NOT A GiRL.
HOW DO YOU KNOW THAT, FOFANA?!
THAT'S ENOUGH, YOU TWO!
iT'S STiLL AN ANiMAL. DON'T HURT iT OR iT MiGHT GET ANGRY AND BiTE YOU.
AND MOST OF ALL, YOU HAVE TO TAKE GREAT CARE OF iT, OK?
YES, MUM. WE'RE GONNA BE NiCE TO HIM. AREN'T WE, AKiSSi?
OH YES, WE'RE GOiNG TO FiND iT A NAME AND EVERYTHiNG.
OUiSTiTi, JUST LiKE iN THE BOOK!
NO, THAT DOESN'T EVEN SOUND NiCE...
BOUBOU!
BOUBOU. VERY NiCE, AKiSSi.
BOUBOU LiKES TO FiND LiCE AND EAT THEM.
BOUBOU, STOP! YOU'RE TiCKLiNG ME!
BA, DO YOU HAVE LiCE??
YOUR MUM'S GONNA SHAVE YOUR HEAD AGAiN.
BOUBOU LiKES TO PLAY WiTH THE BALL.
BOUBOU, GiVE iT BACK!!!
Hi! Hi! Hi!

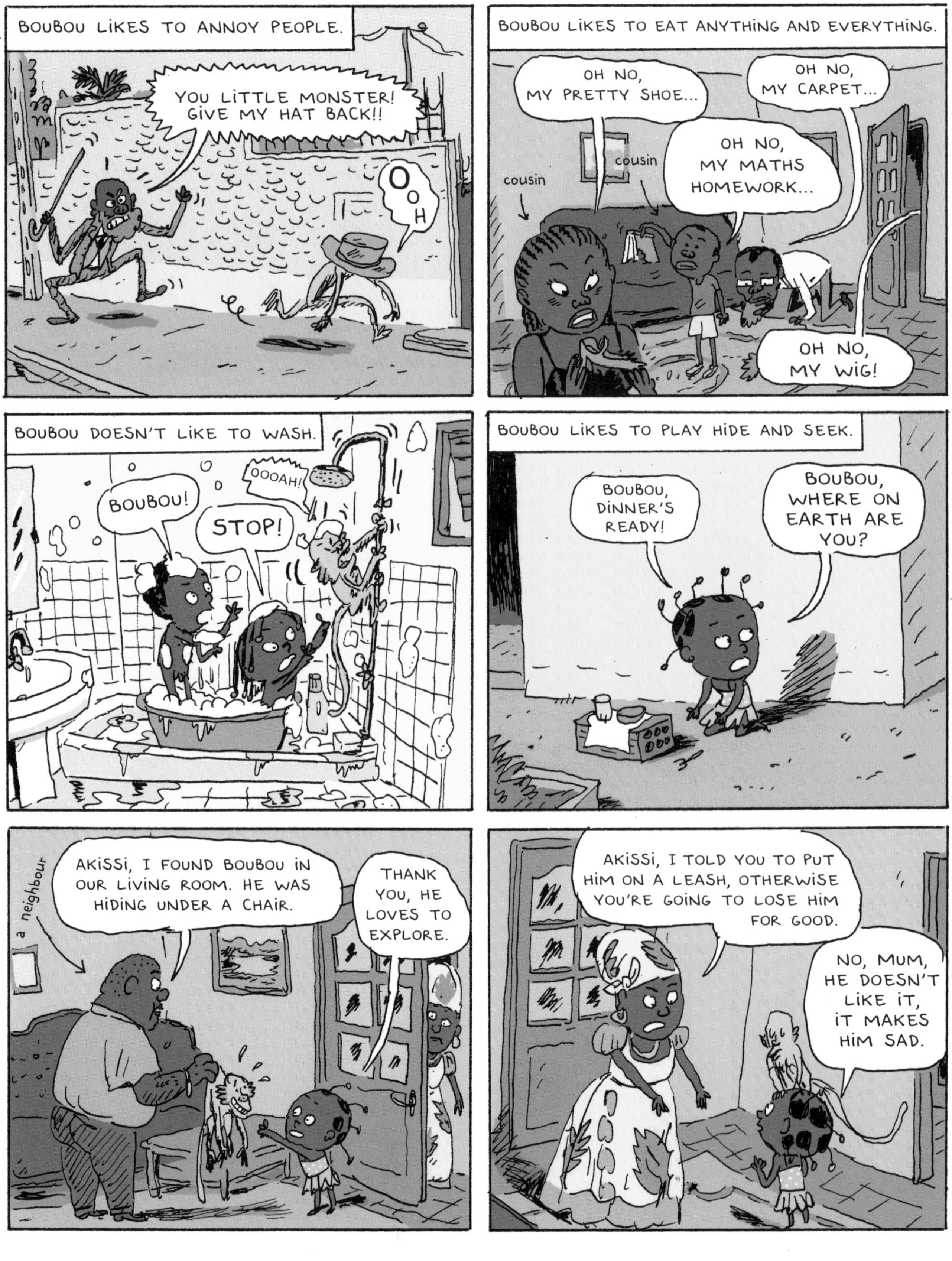
BOUBOU LIKES TO ANNOY PEOPLE.
YOU LITTLE MONSTER! GIVE MY HAT BACK!!
OOH
BOUBOU LIKES TO EAT ANYTHING AND EVERYTHING.
cousin
cousin
OH NO, MY PRETTY SHOE...
OH NO, MY CARPET...
OH NO, MY MATHS HOMEWORK...
OH NO, MY WIG!
BOUBOU DOESN'T LIKE TO WASH.
BOUBOU!
STOP!
OOOAH!
BOUBOU LIKES TO PLAY HIDE AND SEEK.
BOUBOU, DINNER'S READY!
BOUBOU, WHERE ON EARTH ARE YOU?
a neighbour
AKISSI, I FOUND BOUBOU IN OUR LIVING ROOM. HE WAS HIDING UNDER A CHAIR.
THANK YOU, HE LOVES TO EXPLORE.
AKISSI, I TOLD YOU TO PUT HIM ON A LEASH, OTHERWISE YOU'RE GOING TO LOSE HIM FOR GOOD.
NO, MUM, HE DOESN'T LIKE IT, IT MAKES HIM SAD.

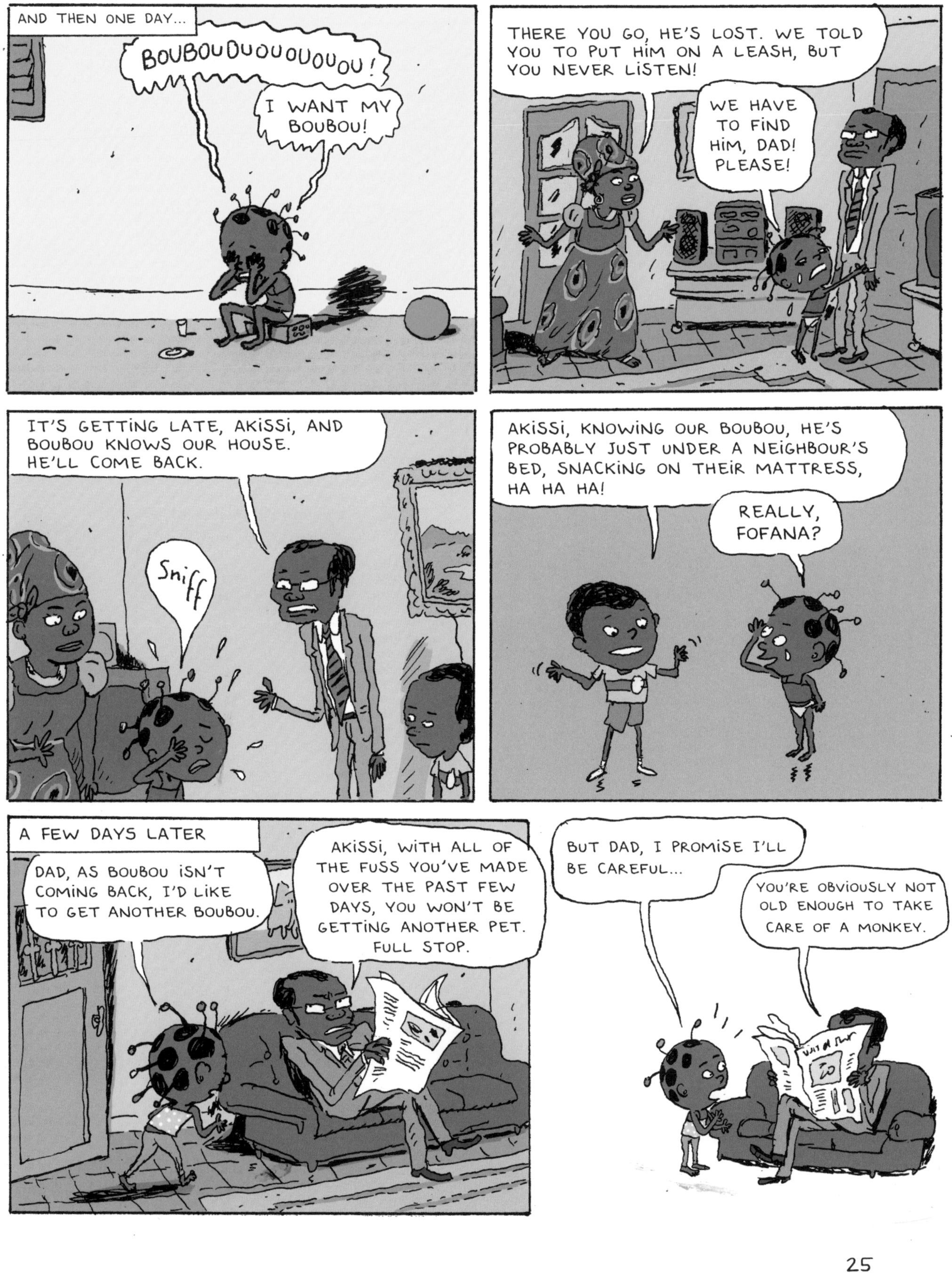
AND THEN ONE DAY...
BOUBOUDUOUOUOUOUOU!
I WANT MY BOUBOU!
THERE YOU GO, HE'S LOST. WE TOLD YOU TO PUT HIM ON A LEASH, BUT YOU NEVER LISTEN!
WE HAVE TO FIND HIM, DAD! PLEASE!
IT'S GETTING LATE, AKISSI, AND BOUBOU KNOWS OUR HOUSE. HE'LL COME BACK.
Sniff
AKISSI, KNOWING OUR BOUBOU, HE'S PROBABLY JUST UNDER A NEIGHBOUR'S BED, SNACKING ON THEIR MATTRESS, HA HA HA!
REALLY, FOFANA?
A FEW DAYS LATER
DAD, AS BOUBOU ISN'T COMING BACK, I'D LIKE TO GET ANOTHER BOUBOU.
AKISSI, WITH ALL OF THE FUSS YOU'VE MADE OVER THE PAST FEW DAYS, YOU WON'T BE GETTING ANOTHER PET. FULL STOP.
BUT DAD, I PROMISE I'LL BE CAREFUL...
YOU'RE OBVIOUSLY NOT OLD ENOUGH TO TAKE CARE OF A MONKEY.

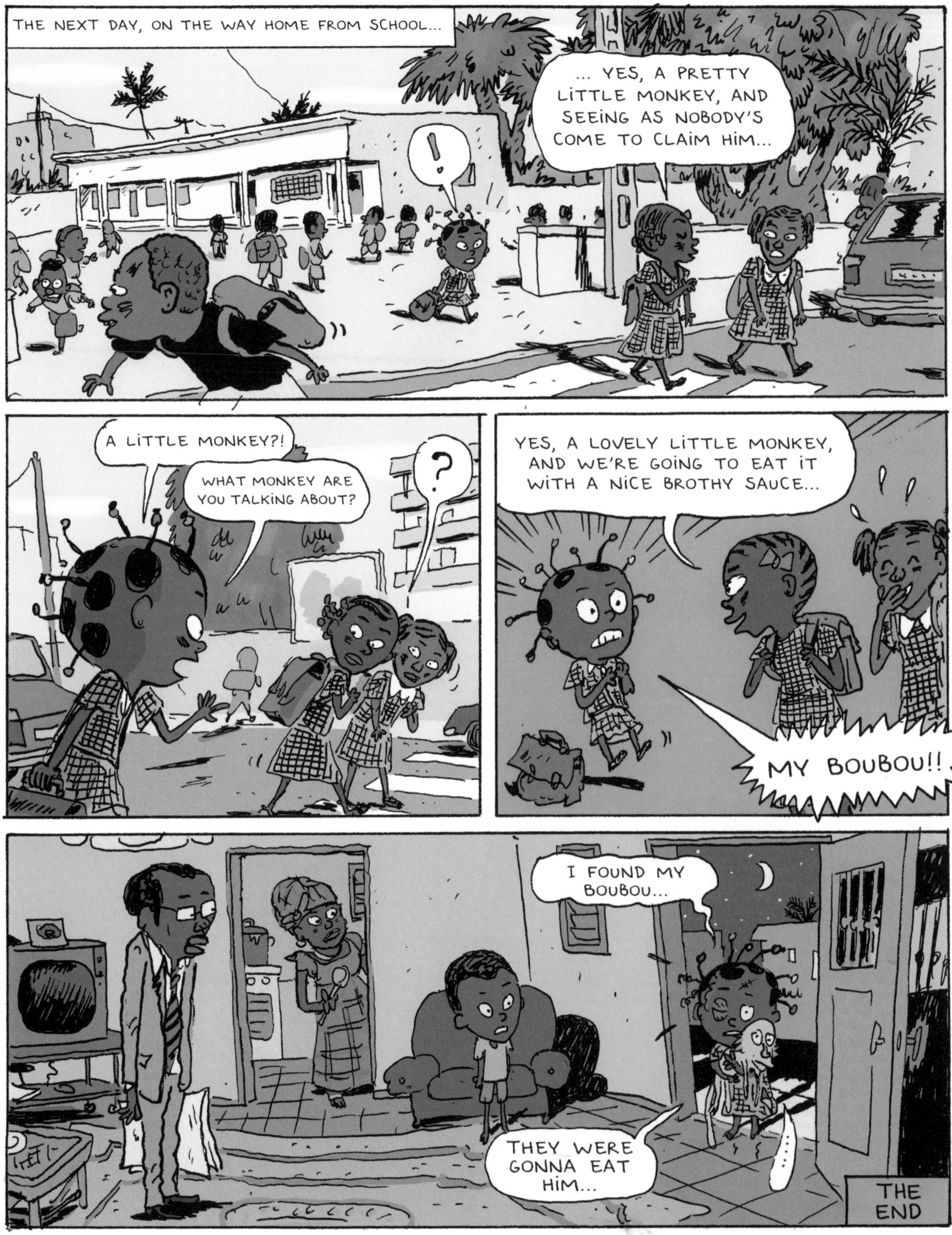
THE NEXT DAY, ON THE WAY HOME FROM SCHOOL...
!
... YES, A PRETTY LITTLE MONKEY, AND SEEING AS NOBODY'S COME TO CLAIM HIM...
A LITTLE MONKEY?!
WHAT MONKEY ARE YOU TALKING ABOUT?
?
YES, A LOVELY LITTLE MONKEY, AND WE'RE GOING TO EAT IT WITH A NICE BROTHY SAUCE...
! !
MY BOUBOU!!
I FOUND MY BOUBOU...
THEY WERE GONNA EAT HIM...
THE END

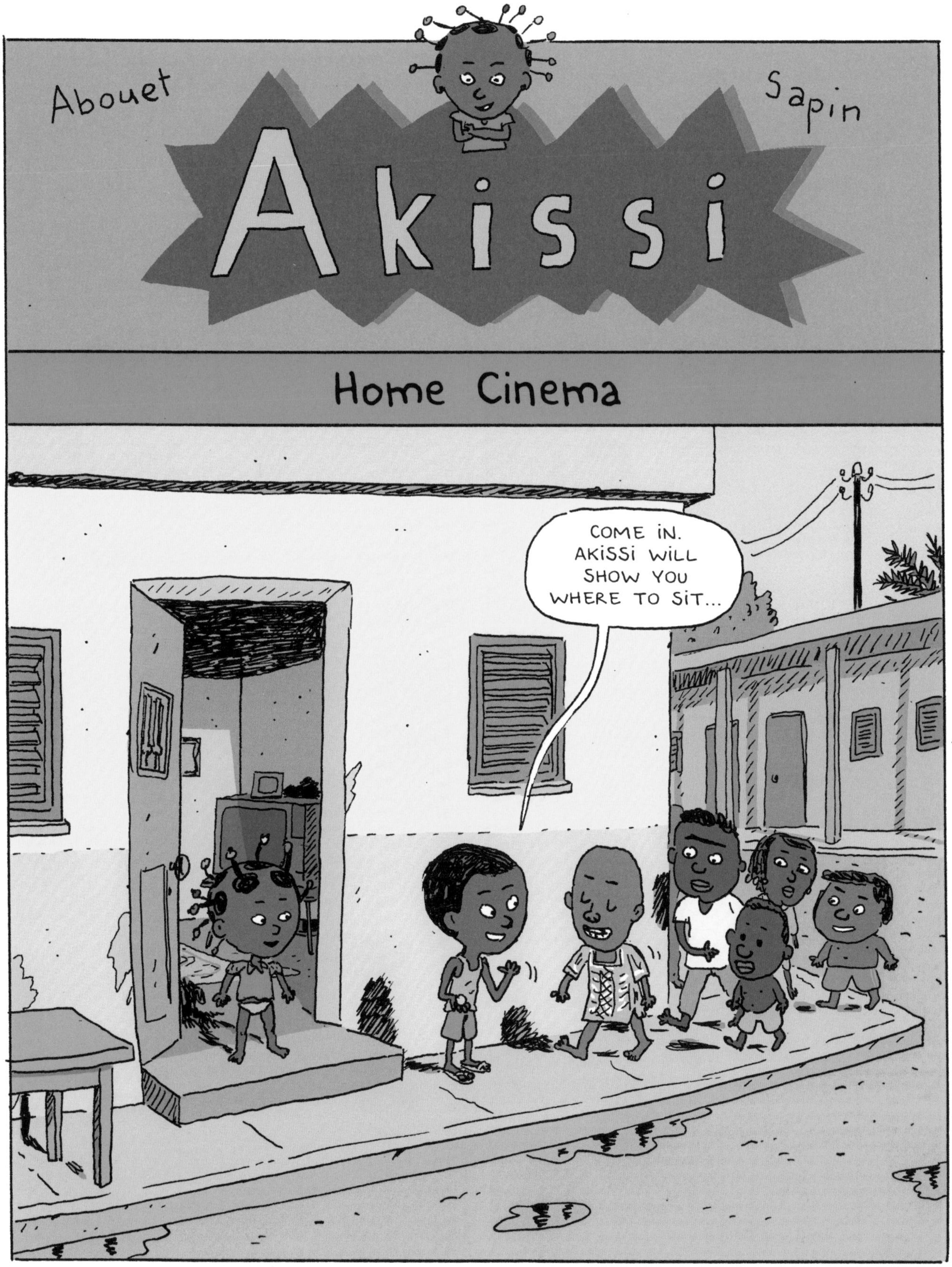
Abouet
Sapin
Akissi
Home Cinema
COME IN. AKISSI WILL SHOW YOU WHERE TO SIT...

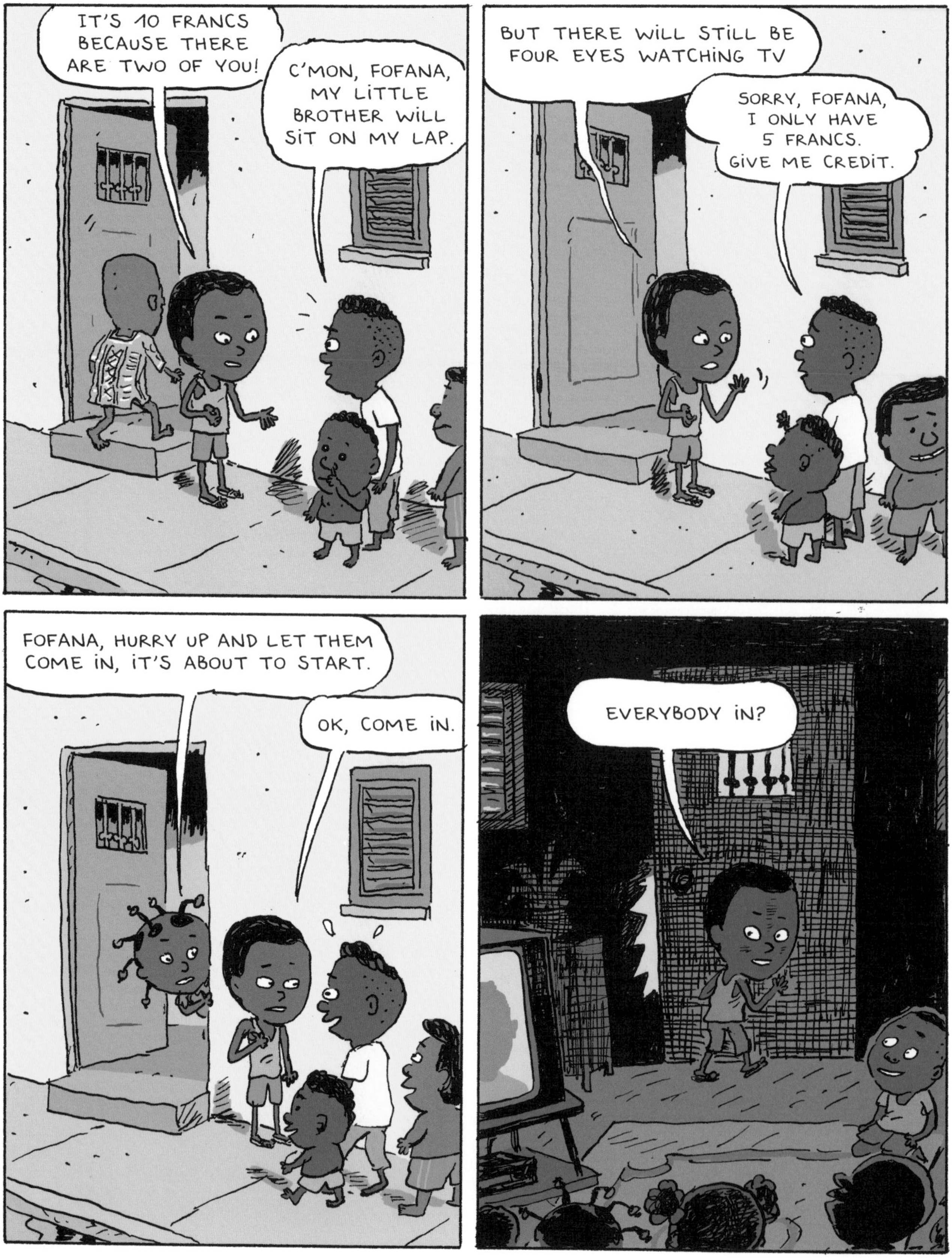
IT'S 10 FRANCS BECAUSE THERE ARE TWO OF YOU!
C'MON, FOFANA, MY LITTLE BROTHER WILL SIT ON MY LAP.
BUT THERE WILL STILL BE FOUR EYES WATCHING TV
SORRY, FOFANA, I ONLY HAVE 5 FRANCS. GIVE ME CREDIT.
FOFANA, HURRY UP AND LET THEM COME IN, IT'S ABOUT TO START.
OK, COME IN.
EVERYBODY IN?

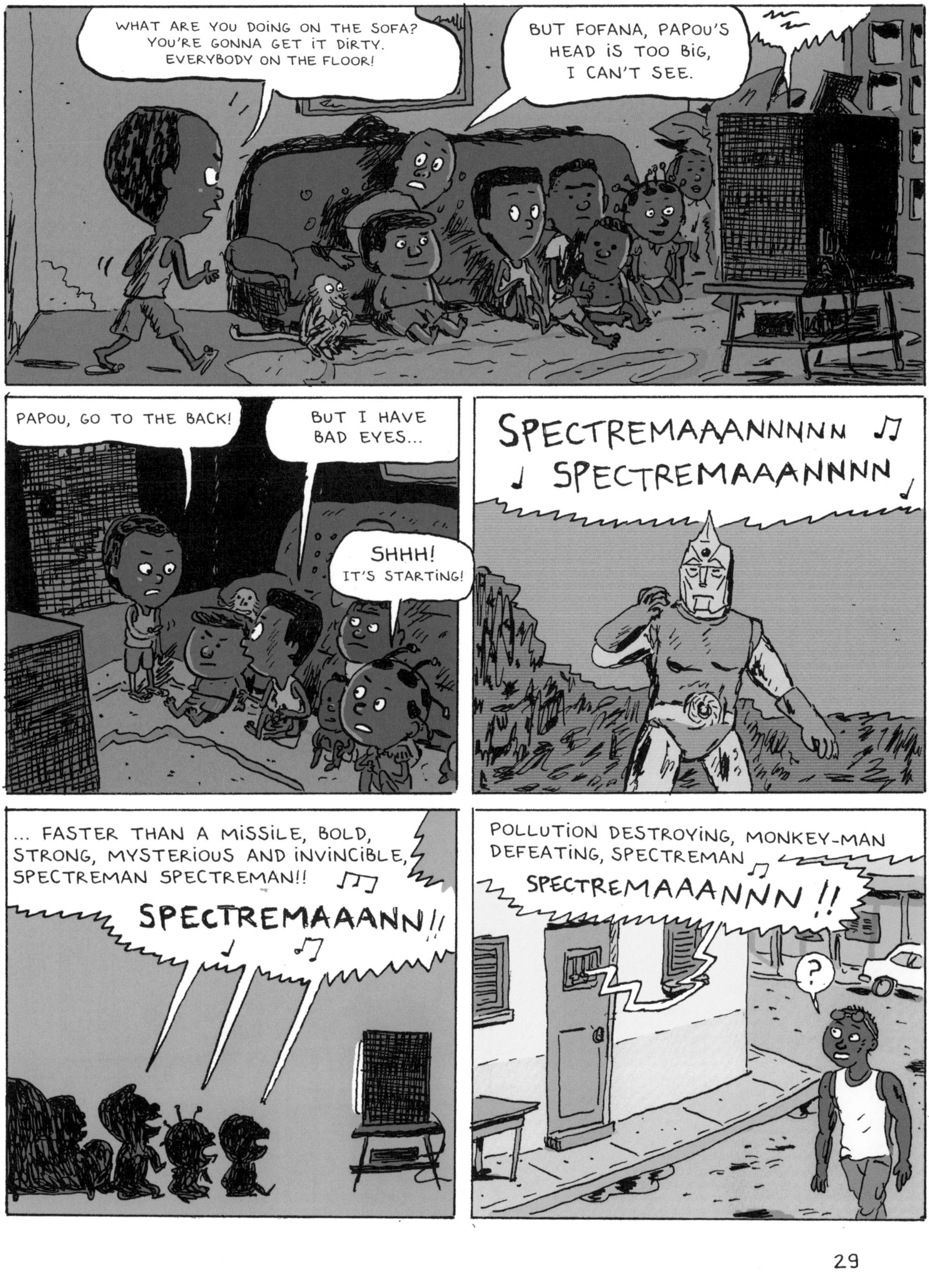
WHAT ARE YOU DOING ON THE SOFA? YOU'RE GONNA GET IT DIRTY. EVERYBODY ON THE FLOOR!
BUT FOFANA, PAPOU'S HEAD IS TOO BIG, I CAN'T SEE.
PAPOU, GO TO THE BACK!
BUT I HAVE BAD EYES...
SHHH! IT'S STARTING!
SPECTREMAAANNNNN SPECTREMAAANNNN
... FASTER THAN A MISSILE, BOLD, STRONG, MYSTERIOUS AND INVINCIBLE, SPECTREMAN SPECTREMAN!!
SPECTREMAAANN!!
POLLUTION DESTROYING, MONKEY-MAN DEFEATING, SPECTREMAN
SPECTREMAAANNN !!
?

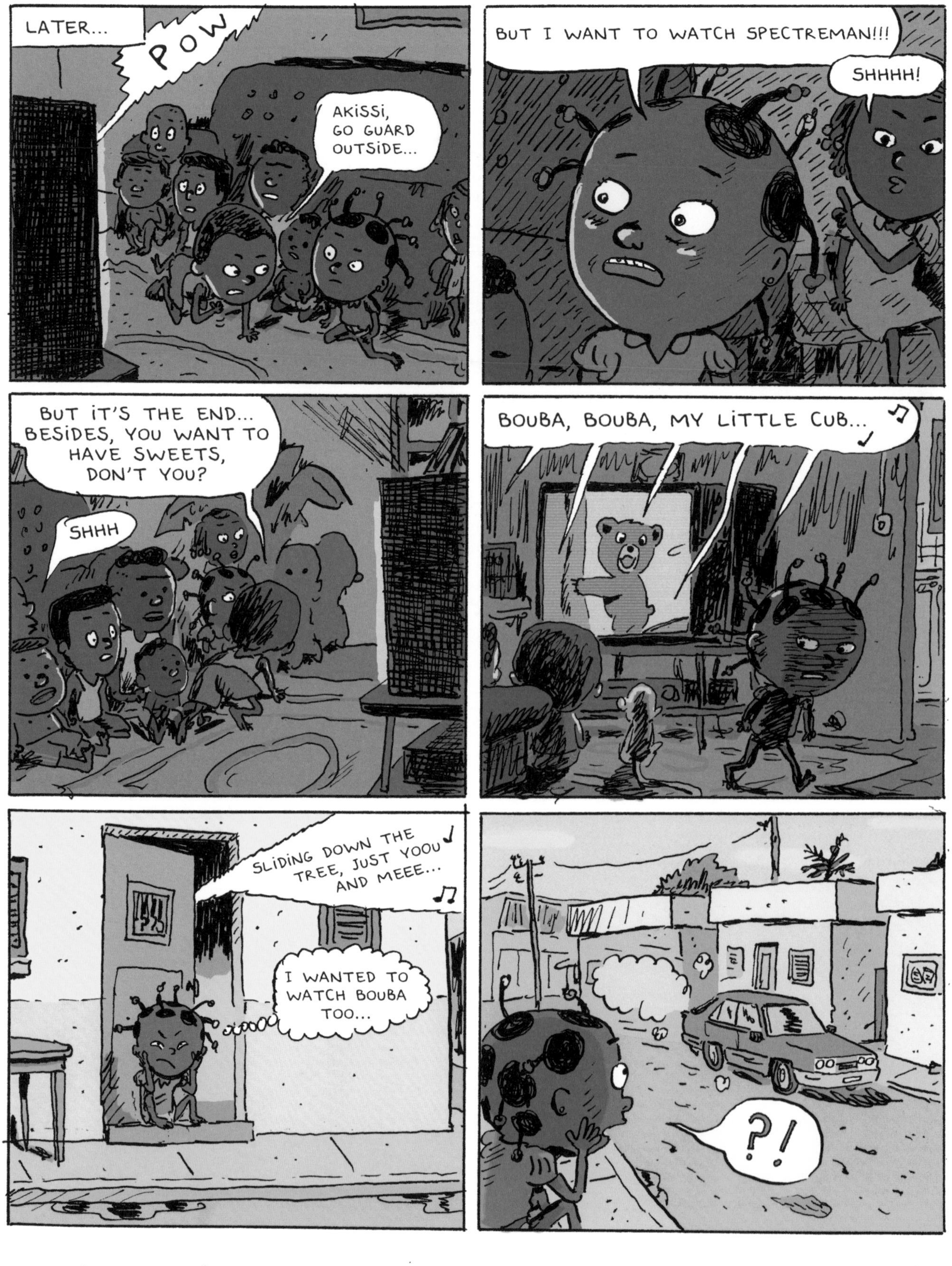

LATER...
POW
AKISSI, GO GUARD OUTSIDE...
BUT I WANT TO WATCH SPECTREMAN!!!
SHHHH!
BUT IT'S THE END... BESIDES, YOU WANT TO HAVE SWEETS, DON'T YOU?
SHHH
BOUBA, BOUBA, MY LITTLE CUB...
SLIDING DOWN THE TREE, JUST YOOU AND MEEE...
I WANTED TO WATCH BOUBA TOO...
?!

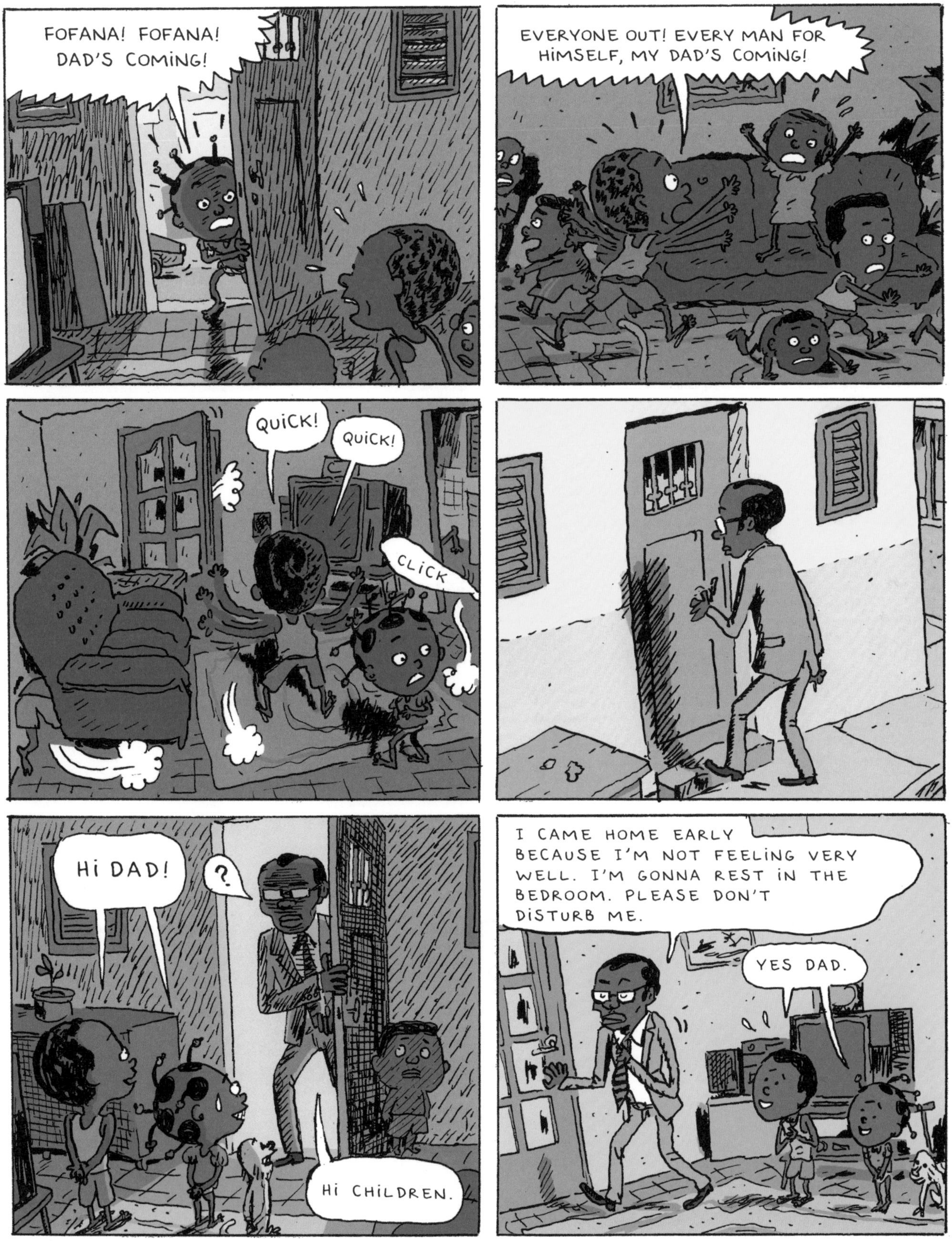

FOFANA! FOFANA! DAD'S COMING!
EVERYONE OUT! EVERY MAN FOR HIMSELF, MY DAD'S COMING!
QUICK!
QUICK!
CLICK
HI DAD!
?
HI CHILDREN.
I CAME HOME EARLY BECAUSE I'M NOT FEELING VERY WELL. I'M GONNA REST IN THE BEDROOM. PLEASE DON'T DISTURB ME.
YES DAD.

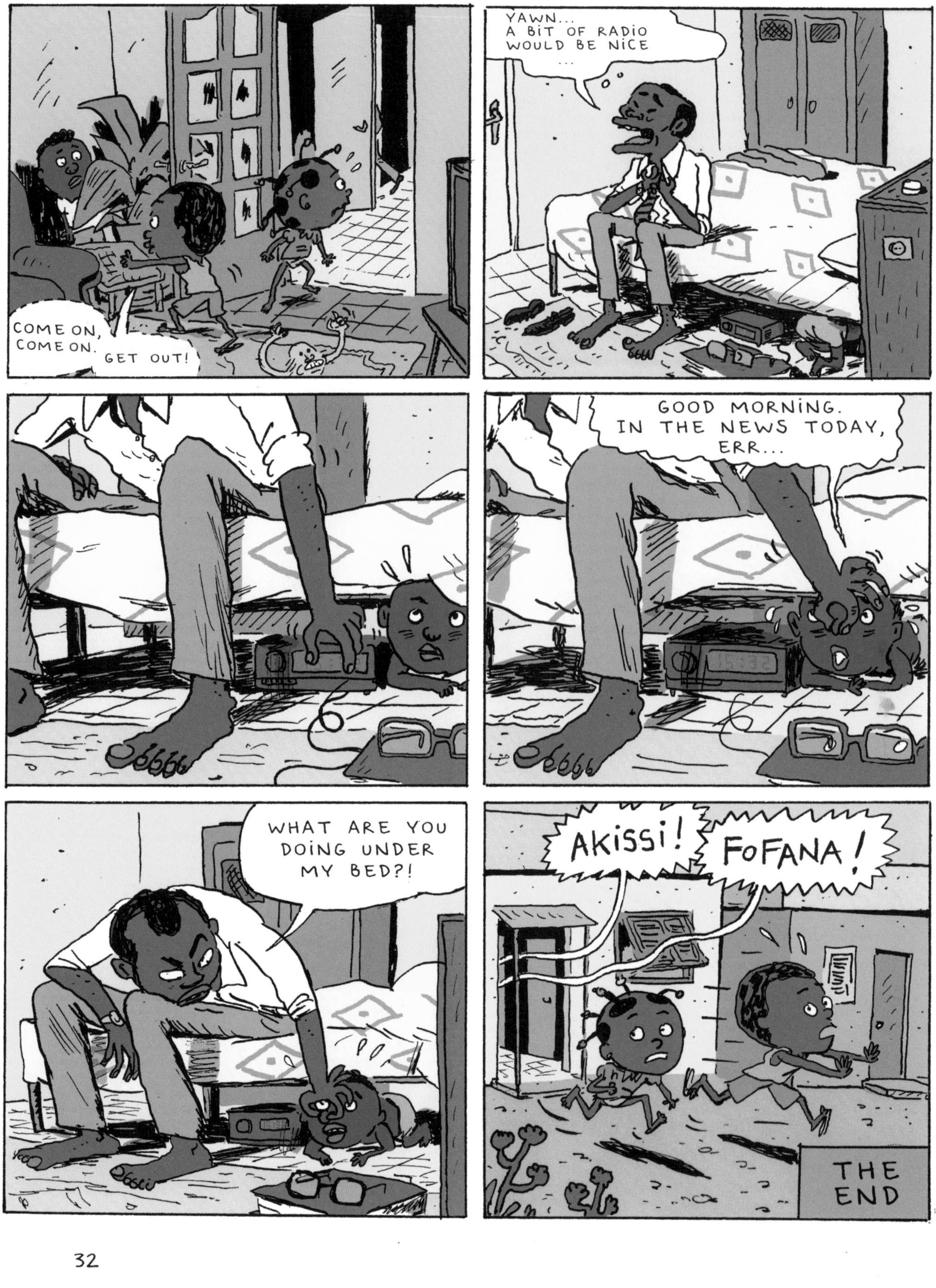
COME ON, COME ON.
GET OUT!
YAWN... A BIT OF RADIO WOULD BE NICE ...
GOOD MORNING. IN THE NEWS TODAY, ERR...
WHAT ARE YOU DOING UNDER MY BED?!
AKISSI!
FOFANA!
THE END

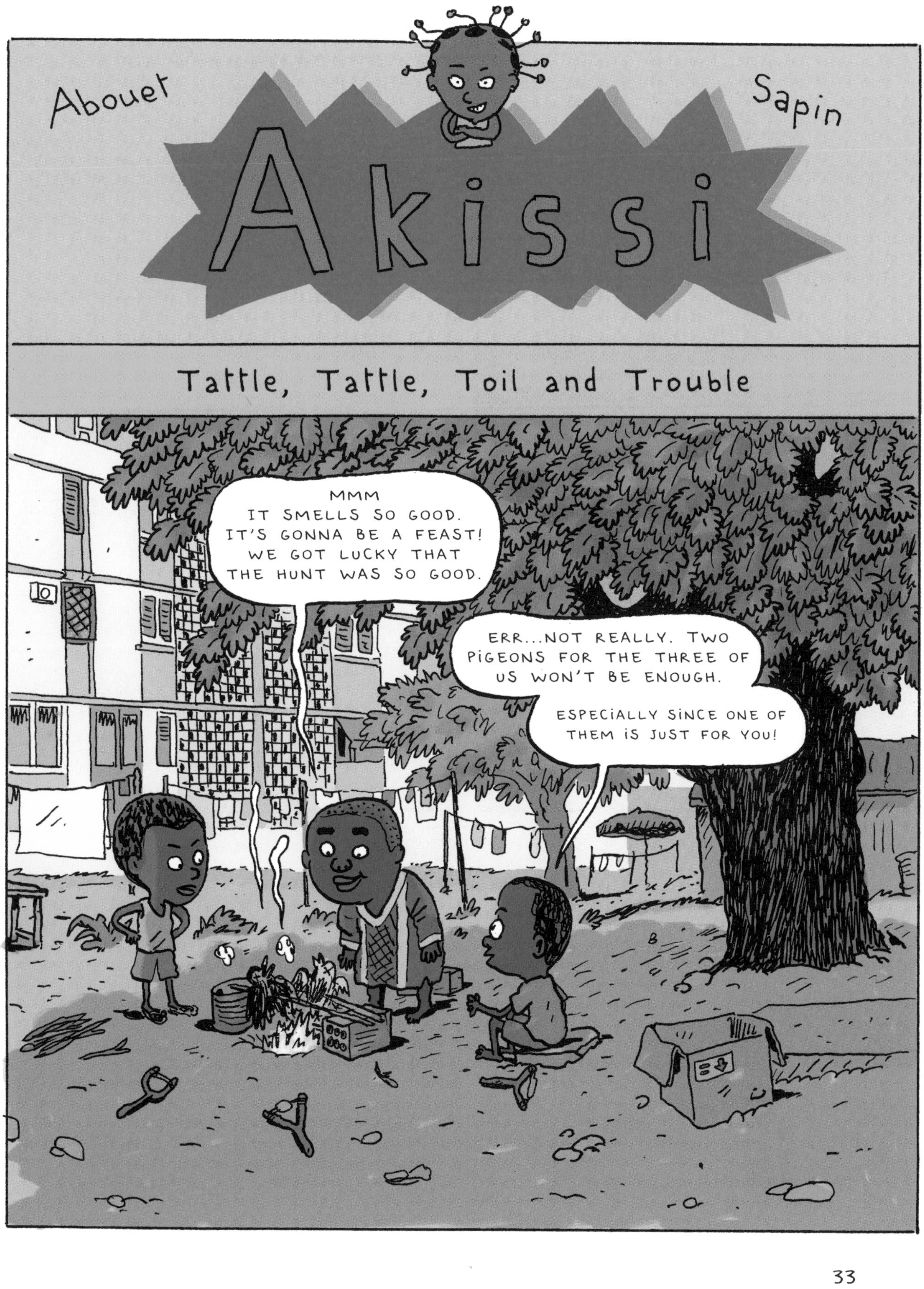
Abouet
Sapin
Akissi
Tattle, Tattle, Toil and Trouble
MMM IT SMELLS SO GOOD. IT'S GONNA BE A FEAST! WE GOT LUCKY THAT THE HUNT WAS SO GOOD.
ERR...NOT REALLY. TWO PIGEONS FOR THE THREE OF US WON'T BE ENOUGH.
ESPECIALLY SINCE ONE OF THEM IS JUST FOR YOU!

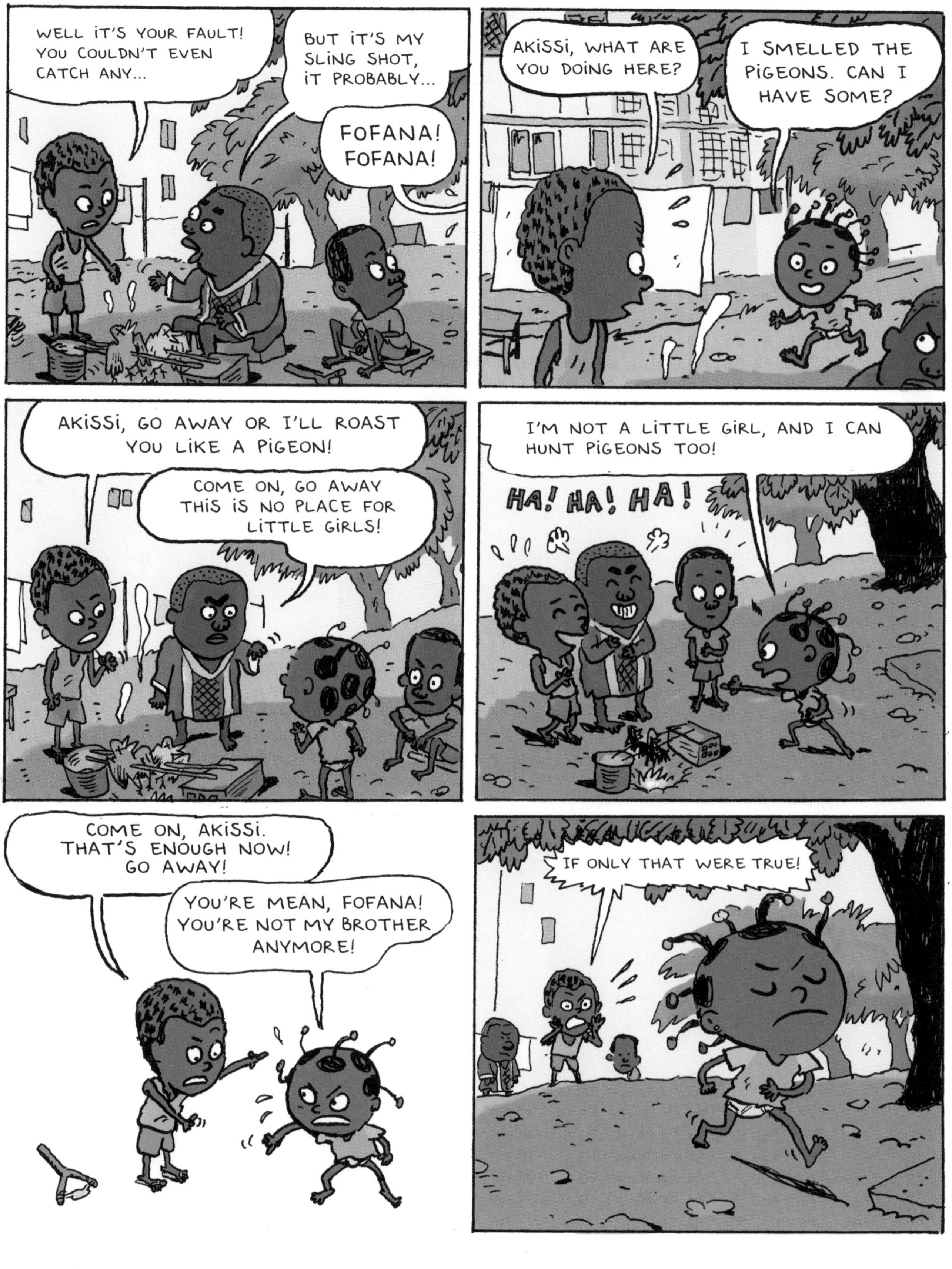
WELL IT'S YOUR FAULT! YOU COULDN'T EVEN CATCH ANY...
BUT IT'S MY SLING SHOT, IT PROBABLY...
FOFANA! FOFANA!
AKISSI, WHAT ARE YOU DOING HERE?
I SMELLED THE PIGEONS. CAN I HAVE SOME?
AKISSI, GO AWAY OR I'LL ROAST YOU LIKE A PIGEON!
COME ON, GO AWAY THIS IS NO PLACE FOR LITTLE GIRLS!
I'M NOT A LITTLE GIRL, AND I CAN HUNT PIGEONS TOO!
HA! HA! HA!
COME ON, AKISSI. THAT'S ENOUGH NOW! GO AWAY!
YOU'RE MEAN, FOFANA! YOU'RE NOT MY BROTHER ANYMORE!
IF ONLY THAT WERE TRUE!

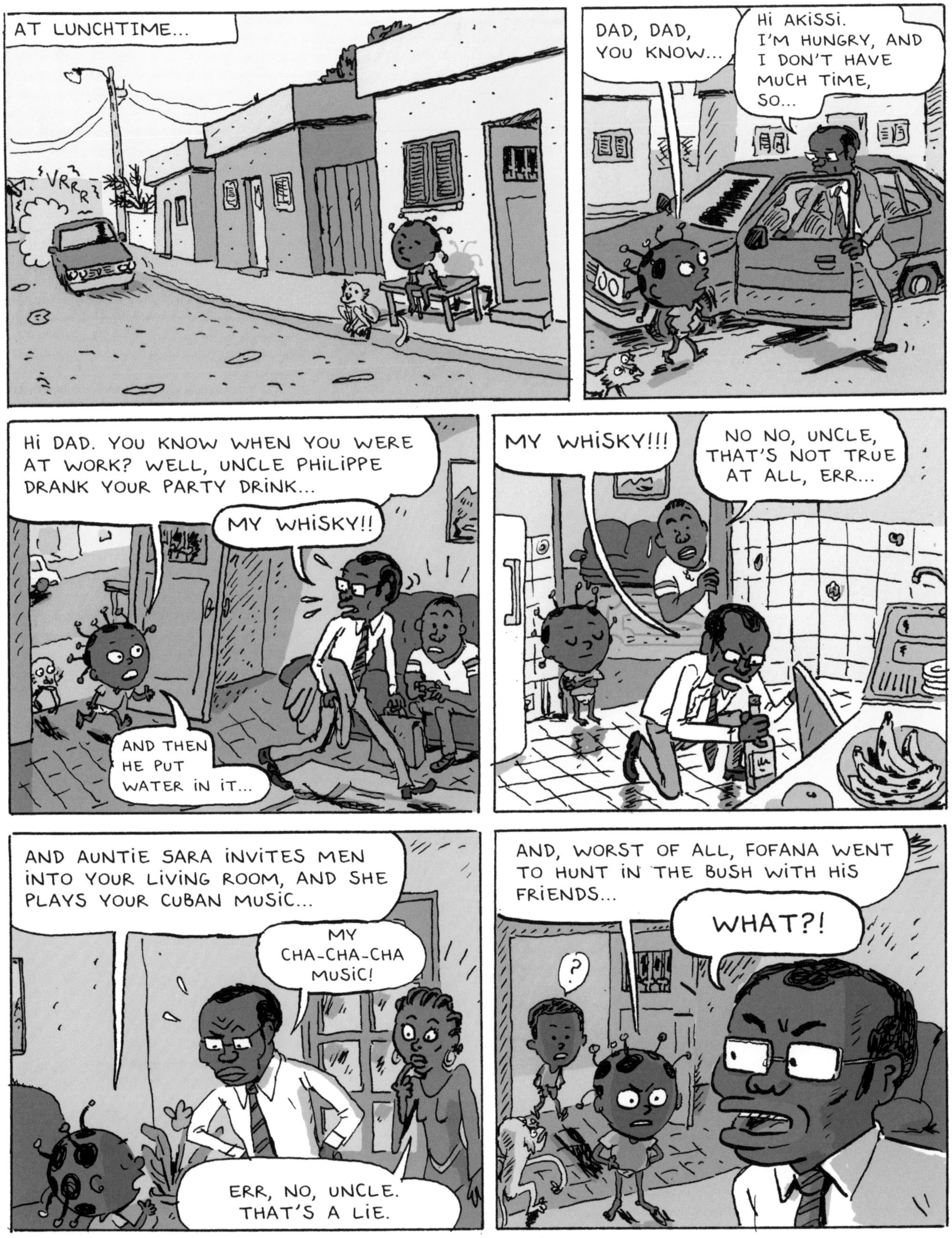
AT LUNCHTIME...
VRRR
DAD, DAD, YOU KNOW...
Hi AKiSSi. I'M HUNGRY, AND I DON'T HAVE MUCH TiME, SO...
Hi DAD. YOU KNOW WHEN YOU WERE AT WORK? WELL, UNCLE PHiLiPPE DRANK YOUR PARTY DRiNK...
MY WHiSKY!!
AND THEN HE PUT WATER iN iT...
MY WHiSKY!!!
NO NO, UNCLE, THAT'S NOT TRUE AT ALL, ERR...
AND AUNTiE SARA iNViTES MEN iNTO YOUR LiViNG ROOM, AND SHE PLAYS YOUR CUBAN MUSiC...
MY CHA-CHA-CHA MUSiC!
ERR, NO, UNCLE. THAT'S A LiE.
AND, WORST OF ALL, FOFANA WENT TO HUNT iN THE BUSH WiTH HiS FRiENDS...
WHAT?!
?

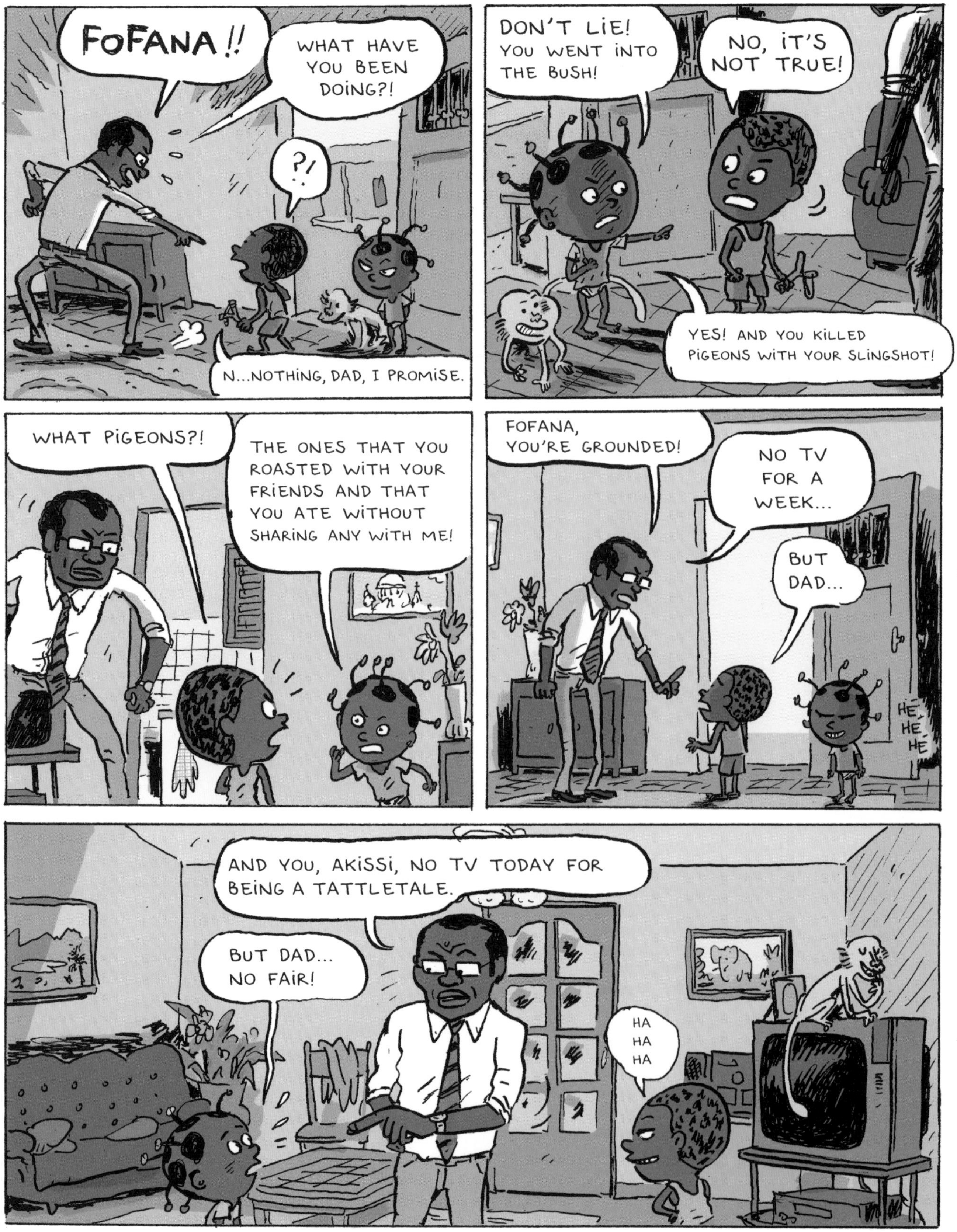
FOFANA!!
WHAT HAVE YOU BEEN DOING?!
?!
N...NOTHING, DAD, I PROMISE.
DON'T LIE! YOU WENT INTO THE BUSH!
NO, IT'S NOT TRUE!
YES! AND YOU KILLED PIGEONS WITH YOUR SLINGSHOT!
WHAT PIGEONS?!
THE ONES THAT YOU ROASTED WITH YOUR FRIENDS AND THAT YOU ATE WITHOUT SHARING ANY WITH ME!
FOFANA, YOU'RE GROUNDED!
NO TV FOR A WEEK...
BUT DAD...
HE HE HE
AND YOU, AKISSI, NO TV TODAY FOR BEING A TATTLETALE.
BUT DAD... NO FAIR!
HA HA HA

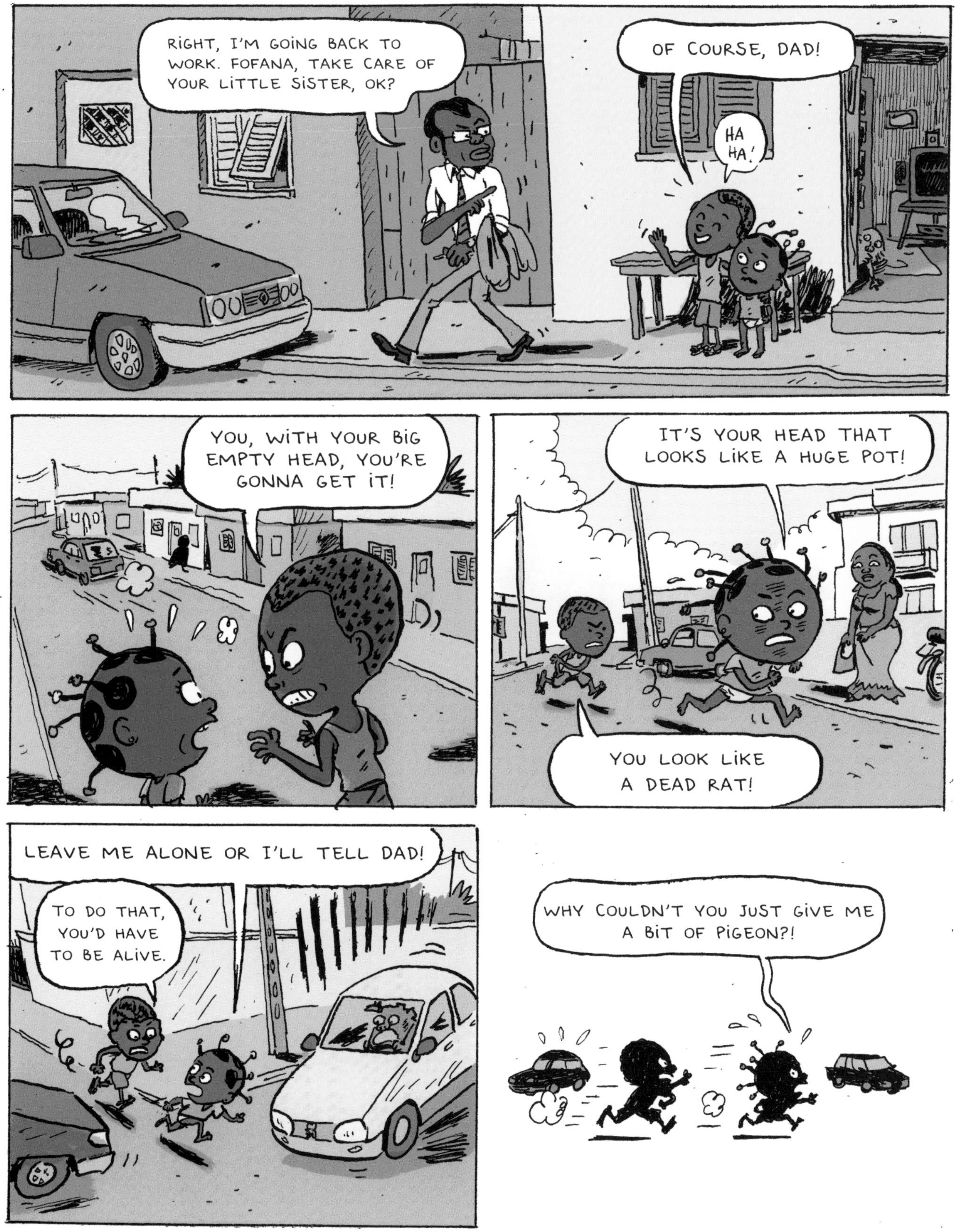
RIGHT, I'M GOING BACK TO WORK. FOFANA, TAKE CARE OF YOUR LITTLE SISTER, OK?
OF COURSE, DAD!
HA HA!
YOU, WITH YOUR BIG EMPTY HEAD, YOU'RE GONNA GET IT!
IT'S YOUR HEAD THAT LOOKS LIKE A HUGE POT!
YOU LOOK LIKE A DEAD RAT!
LEAVE ME ALONE OR I'LL TELL DAD!
TO DO THAT, YOU'D HAVE TO BE ALIVE.
WHY COULDN'T YOU JUST GIVE ME A BIT OF PIGEON?!

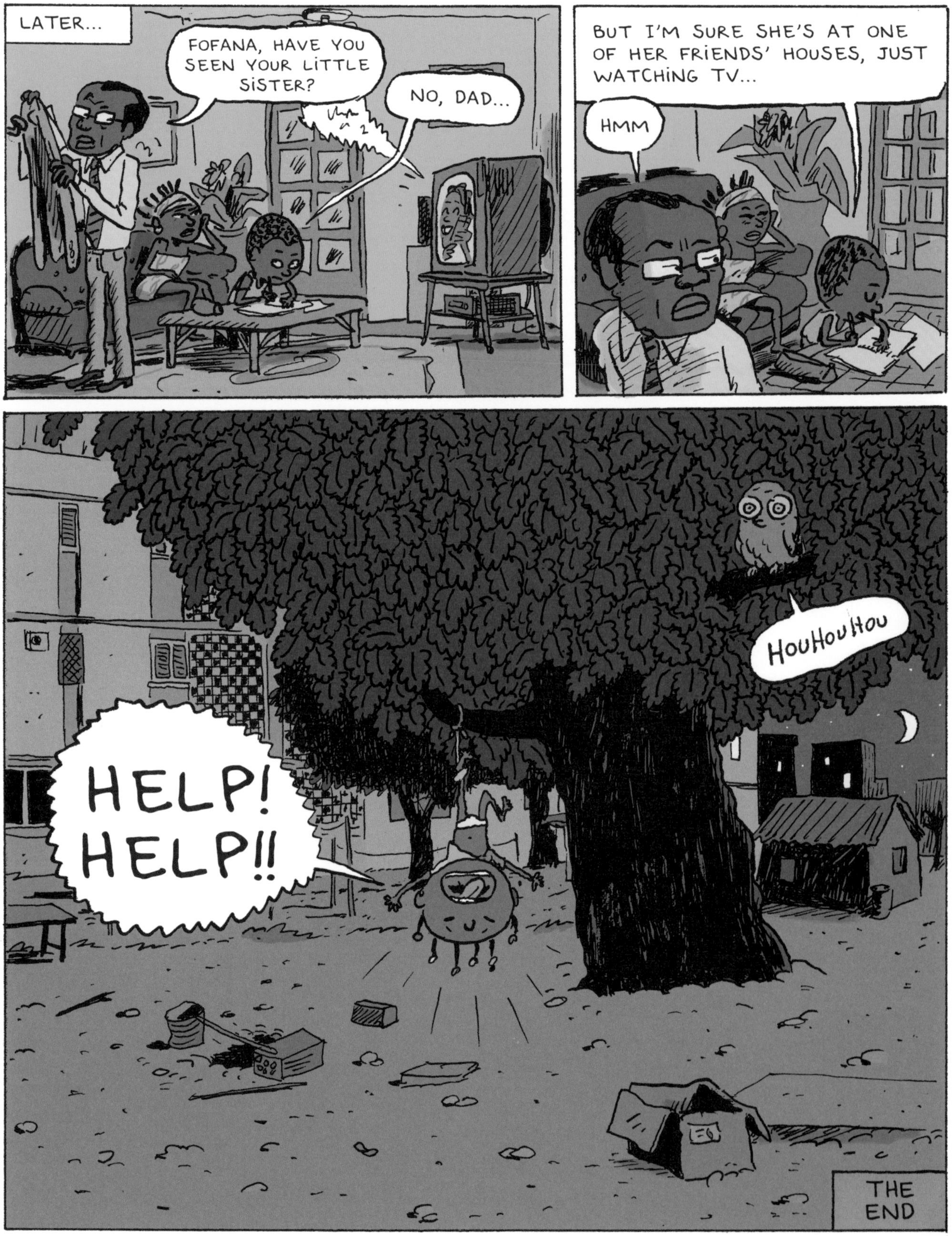
LATER...
FOFANA, HAVE YOU SEEN YOUR LITTLE SISTER?
NO, DAD...
BUT I'M SURE SHE'S AT ONE OF HER FRIENDS' HOUSES, JUST WATCHING TV...
HMM
HouHouHou
HELP! HELP!!
THE END

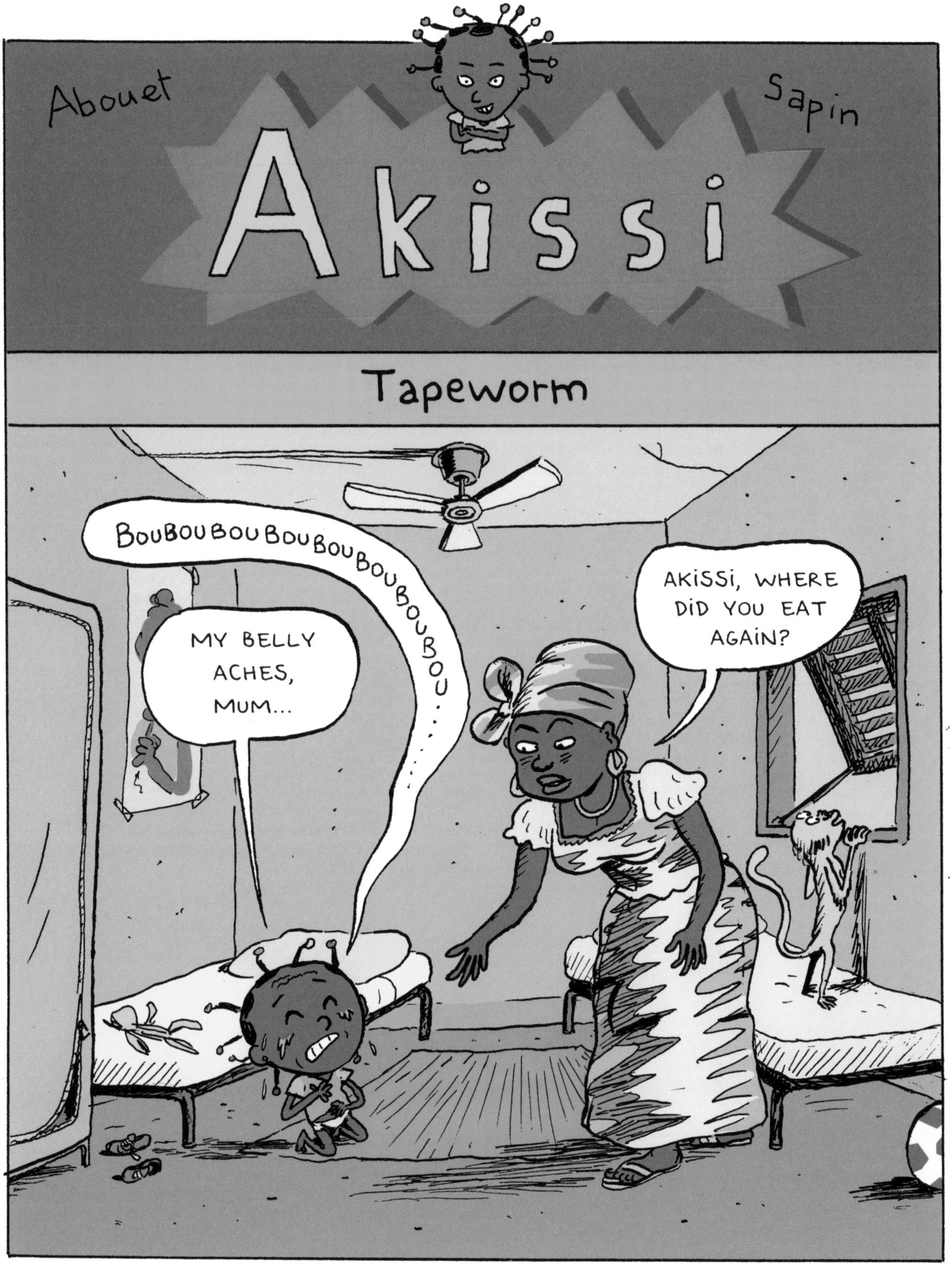

Abouet
Sapin
Akissi
Tapeworm
BOUBOUBOUBOUBOUBOUBOUBOUBOU...
MY BELLY ACHES, MUM...
AKISSI, WHERE DID YOU EAT AGAIN?

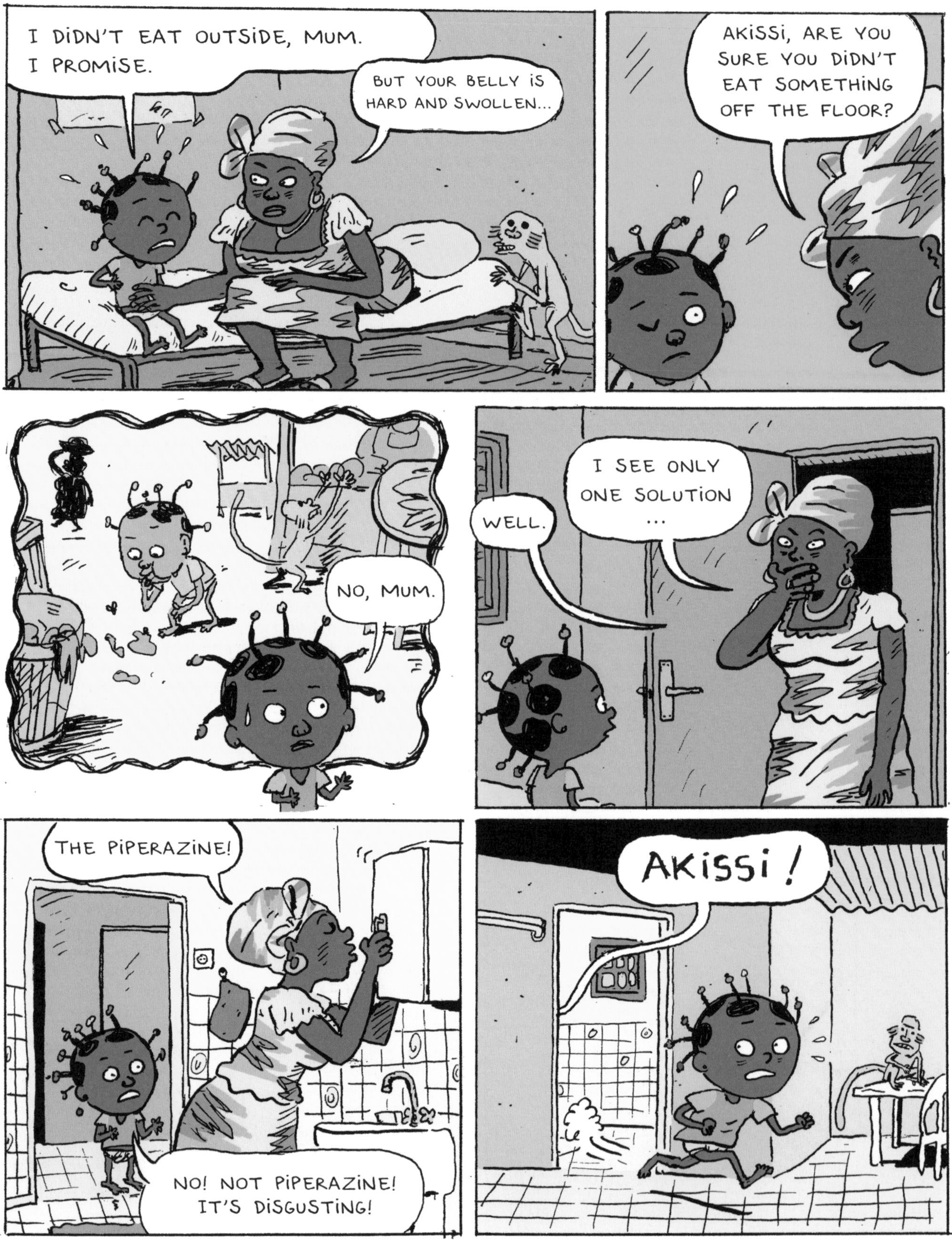

I DIDN'T EAT OUTSIDE, MUM. I PROMISE.
BUT YOUR BELLY IS HARD AND SWOLLEN...
AKISSI, ARE YOU SURE YOU DIDN'T EAT SOMETHING OFF THE FLOOR?
NO, MUM.
WELL.
I SEE ONLY ONE SOLUTION ...
THE PIPERAZINE!
NO! NOT PIPERAZINE! IT'S DISGUSTING!
AKISSI !

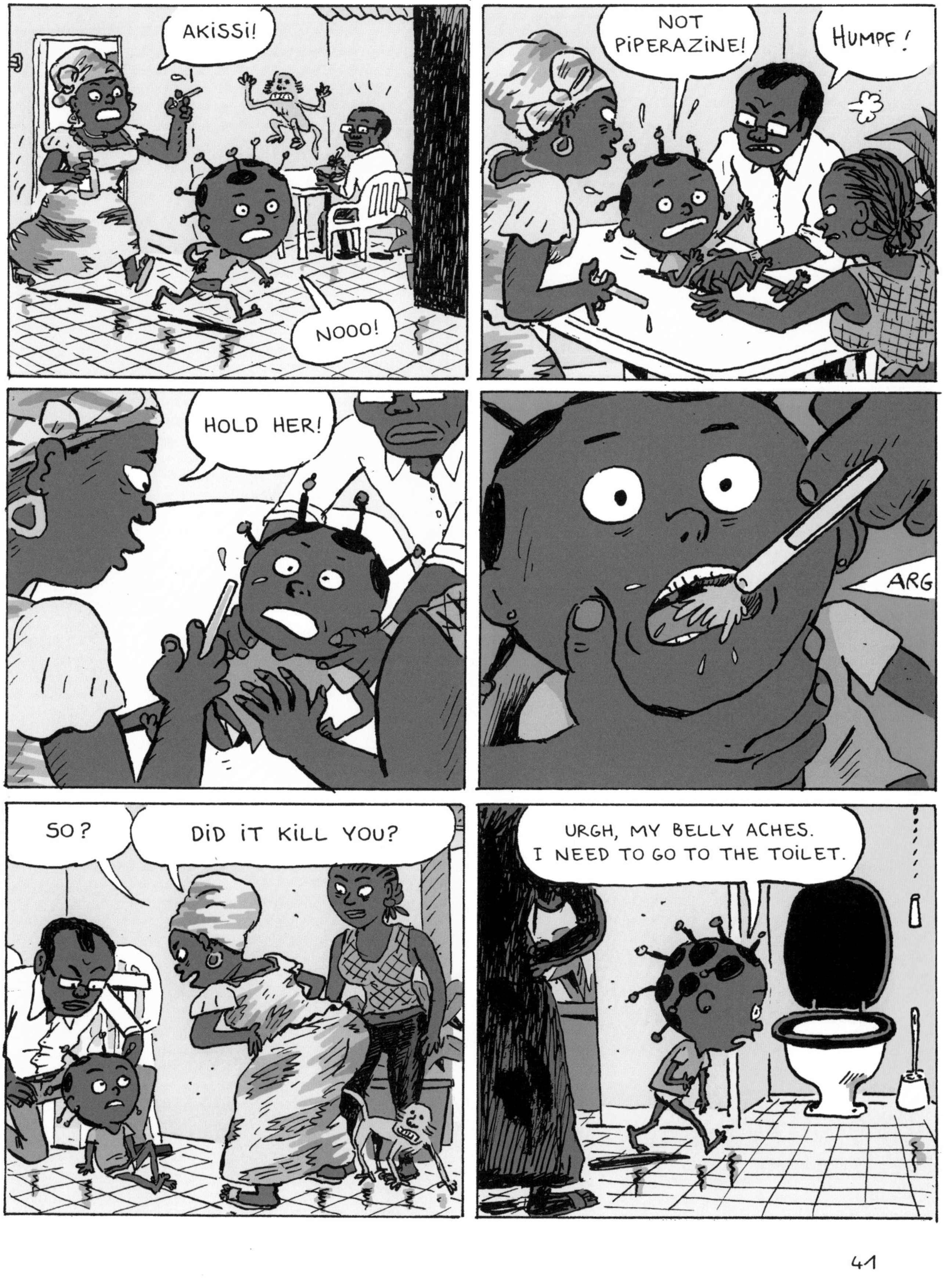
AKISSI!
NOOO!
NOT PIPERAZINE!
HUMPF!
HOLD HER!
ARG
SO?
DID IT KILL YOU?
URGH, MY BELLY ACHES. I NEED TO GO TO THE TOILET.

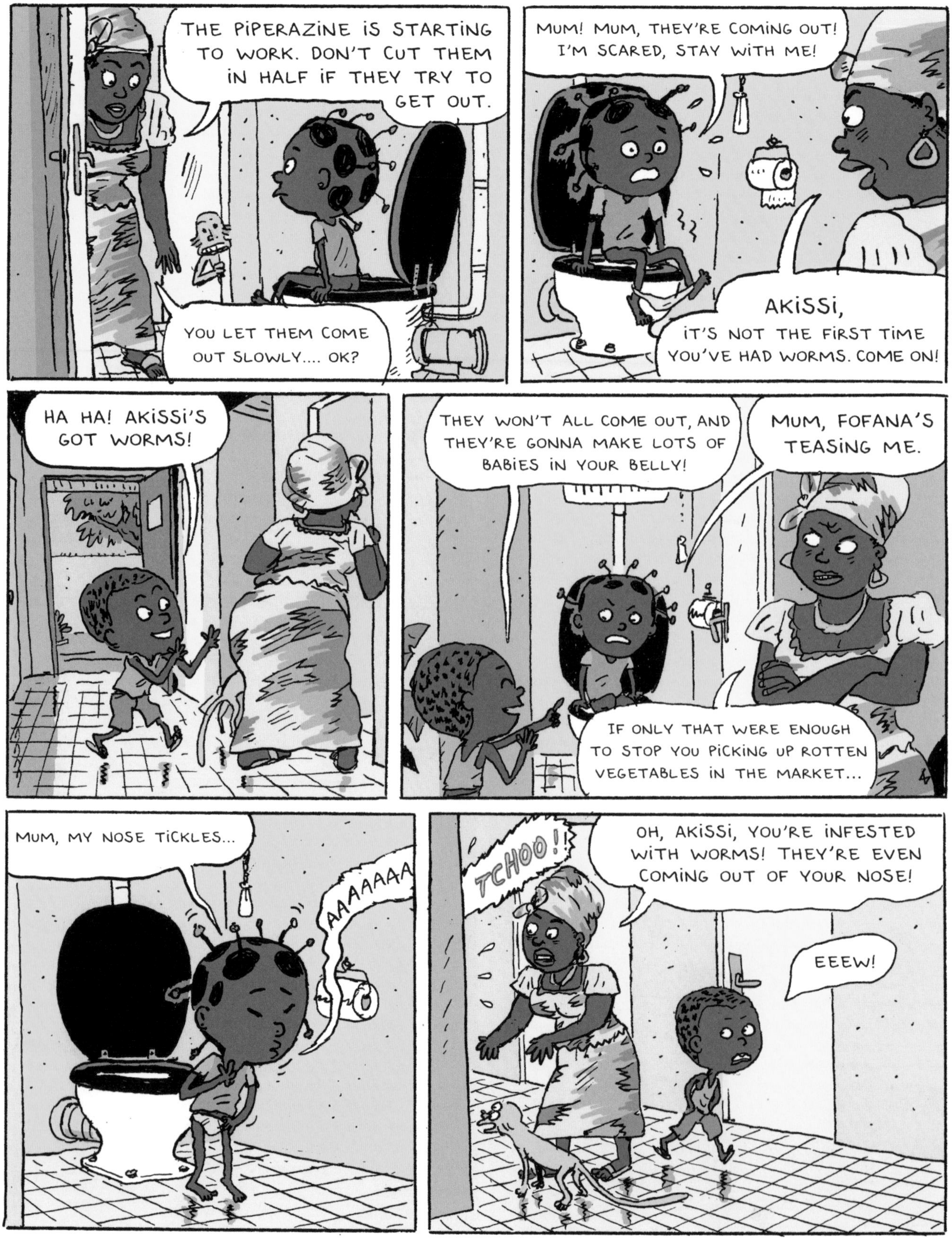
THE PIPERAZINE IS STARTING TO WORK. DON'T CUT THEM IN HALF IF THEY TRY TO GET OUT.
YOU LET THEM COME OUT SLOWLY.... OK?
MUM! MUM, THEY'RE COMING OUT! I'M SCARED, STAY WITH ME!
AKISSI, IT'S NOT THE FIRST TIME YOU'VE HAD WORMS. COME ON!
HA HA! AKISSI'S GOT WORMS!
THEY WON'T ALL COME OUT, AND THEY'RE GONNA MAKE LOTS OF BABIES IN YOUR BELLY!
MUM, FOFANA'S TEASING ME.
IF ONLY THAT WERE ENOUGH TO STOP YOU PICKING UP ROTTEN VEGETABLES IN THE MARKET...
MUM, MY NOSE TICKLES...
AAAAAAA
TCHOO!!
OH, AKISSI, YOU'RE INFESTED WITH WORMS! THEY'RE EVEN COMING OUT OF YOUR NOSE!
EEEW!

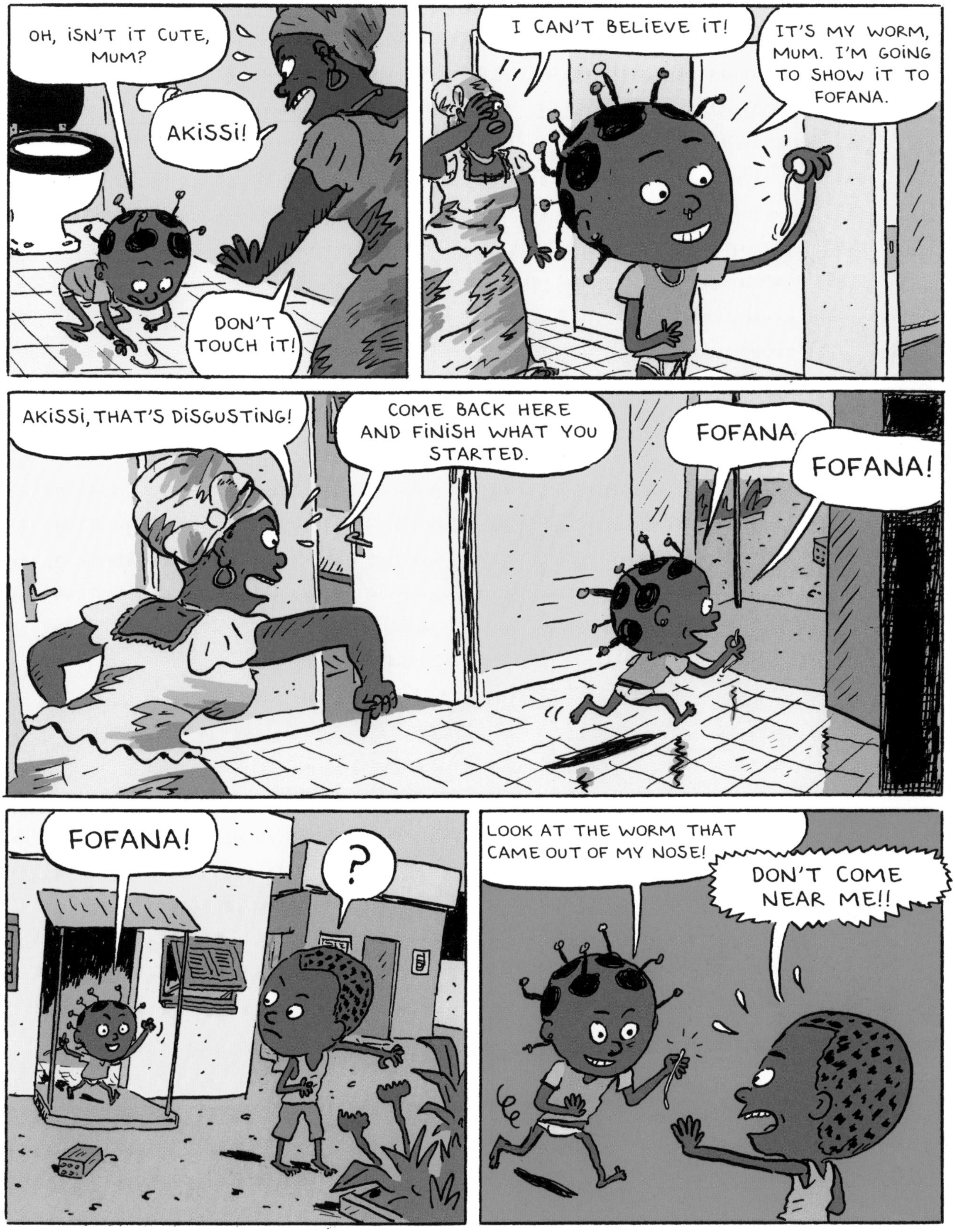

OH, ISN'T IT CUTE, MUM?
AKISSI!
DON'T TOUCH IT!
I CAN'T BELIEVE IT!
IT'S MY WORM, MUM. I'M GOING TO SHOW IT TO FOFANA.
AKISSI, THAT'S DISGUSTING!
COME BACK HERE AND FINISH WHAT YOU STARTED.
FOFANA
FOFANA!
FOFANA!
?
LOOK AT THE WORM THAT CAME OUT OF MY NOSE!
DON'T COME NEAR ME!!

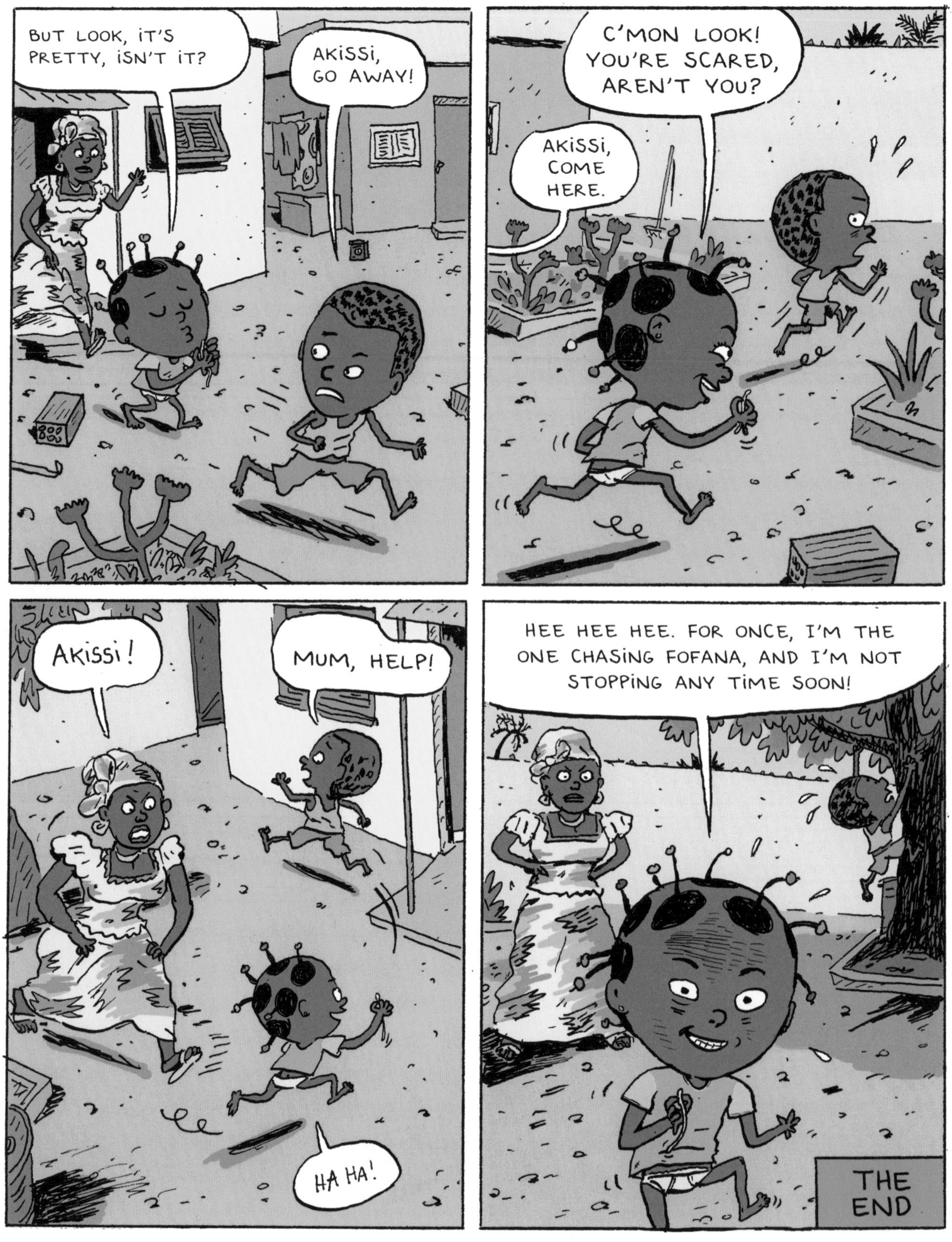
BUT LOOK, IT'S PRETTY, ISN'T IT?
AKISSI, GO AWAY!
C'MON LOOK! YOU'RE SCARED, AREN'T YOU?
AKISSI, COME HERE.
AKISSI!
MUM, HELP!
HA HA!
HEE HEE HEE. FOR ONCE, I'M THE ONE CHASING FOFANA, AND I'M NOT STOPPING ANY TIME SOON!
THE END

BONUS

RECIPE!

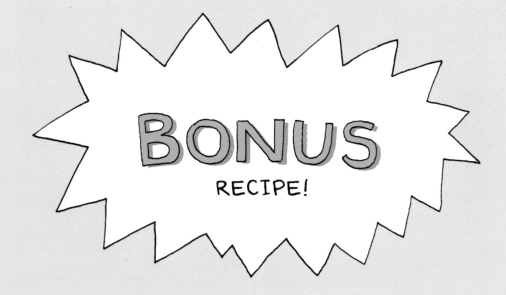

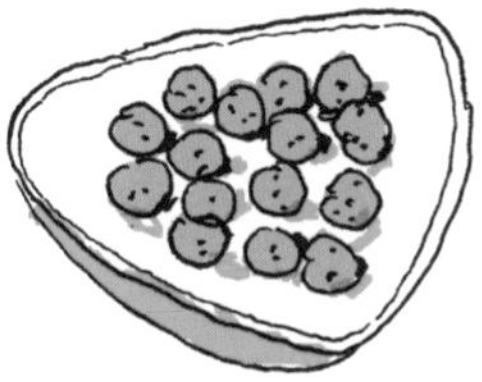

COCONUT GOAT'S DROPPINGS
for all of my friends

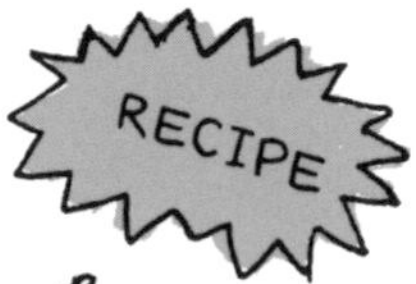
RECIPE

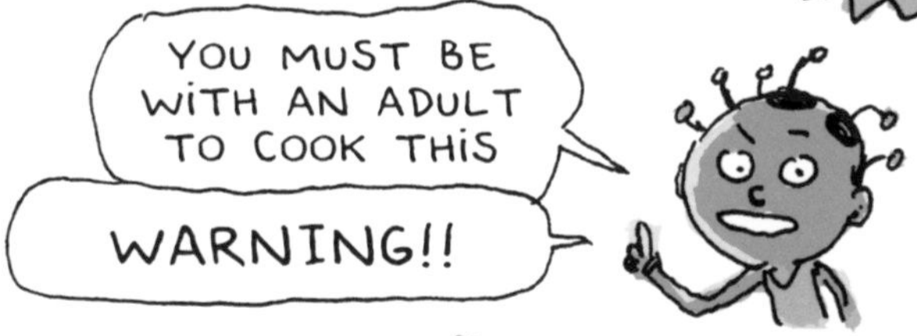
YOU MUST BE WITH AN ADULT TO COOK THIS
WARNING!!

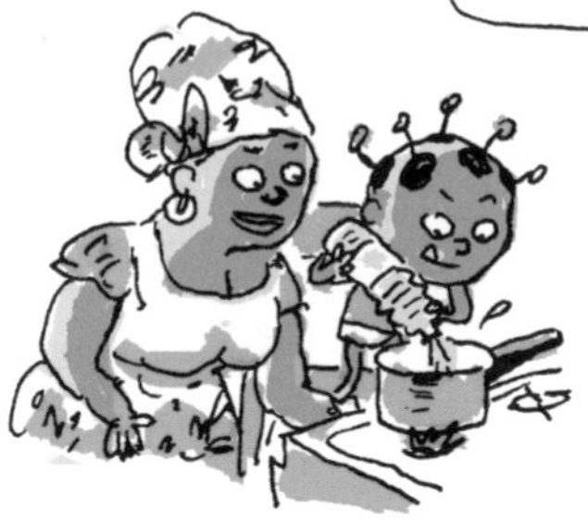

INGREDIENTS for 10 people:

- a can of sweet condensed milk (397g)
- coconut shavings (50g)
- sunflower oil

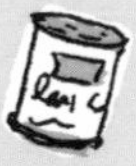

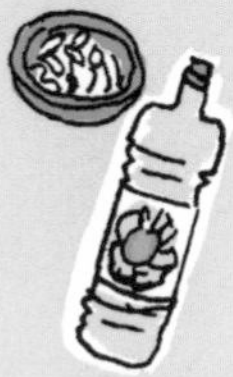

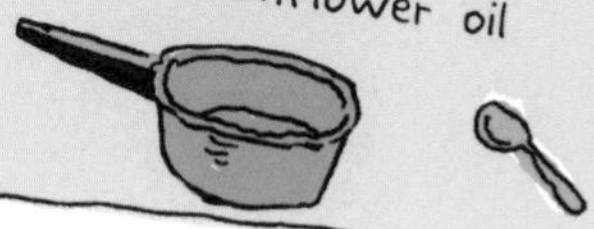

PREPARATION TIME: about 10 minutes

(1) First, convince an adult to help you by telling them they'll get to eat some too.

(2) Put 2 tablespoons of sunflower oil in a pan. (Warning: never use a stove on your own! Always ask an adult to help.) Heat the oil, then pour in the milk and stir for 5 minutes.

(3) When the milk starts to turn brown, drop in the coconut shavings and stir for another 5 minutes, making sure that the mix doesn't stick to the bottom of the pan.

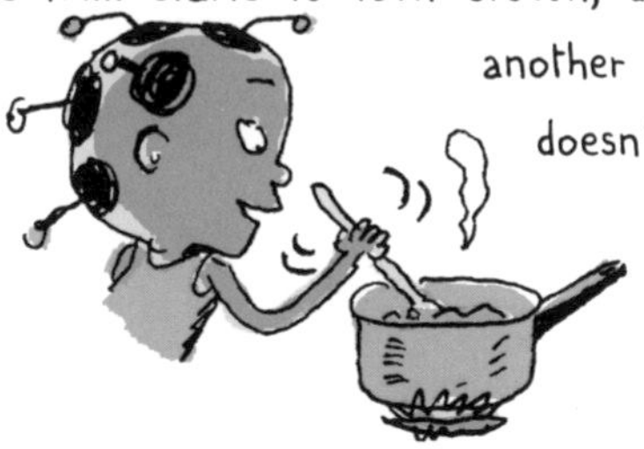

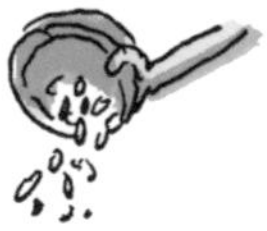

(4) When the mix becomes brown and turns into a soft dough (a bit like mash), pour it onto a plate. Then let it cool down a bit and make balls out of the dough by rolling it in your hands. (But be careful – don't burn yourself!)

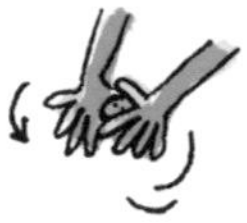

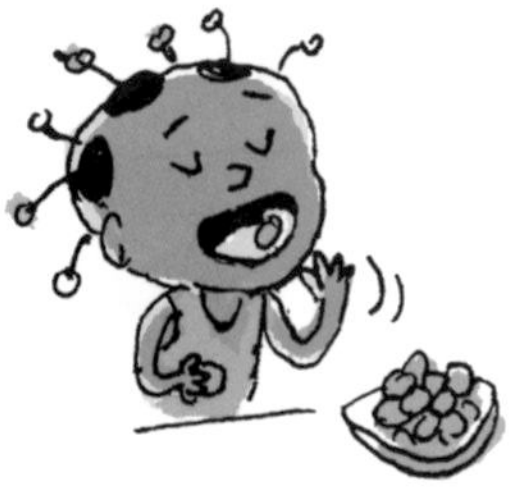

(5) There you go! You can now munch your coconut goat droppings with your friends. When they're warm, they're all soft. Cold, they get harder and are super-tasty.

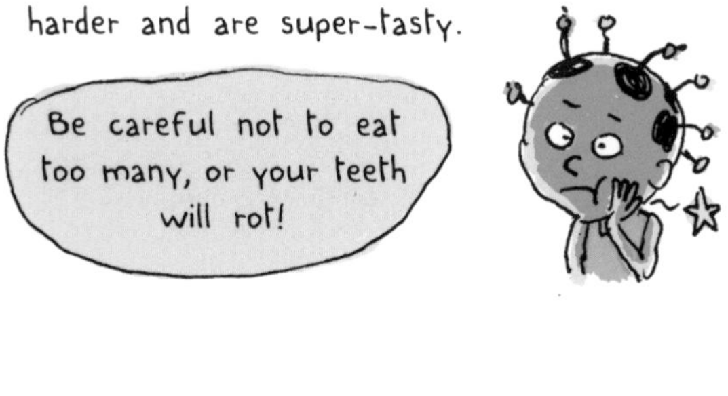
Be careful not to eat too many, or your teeth will rot!

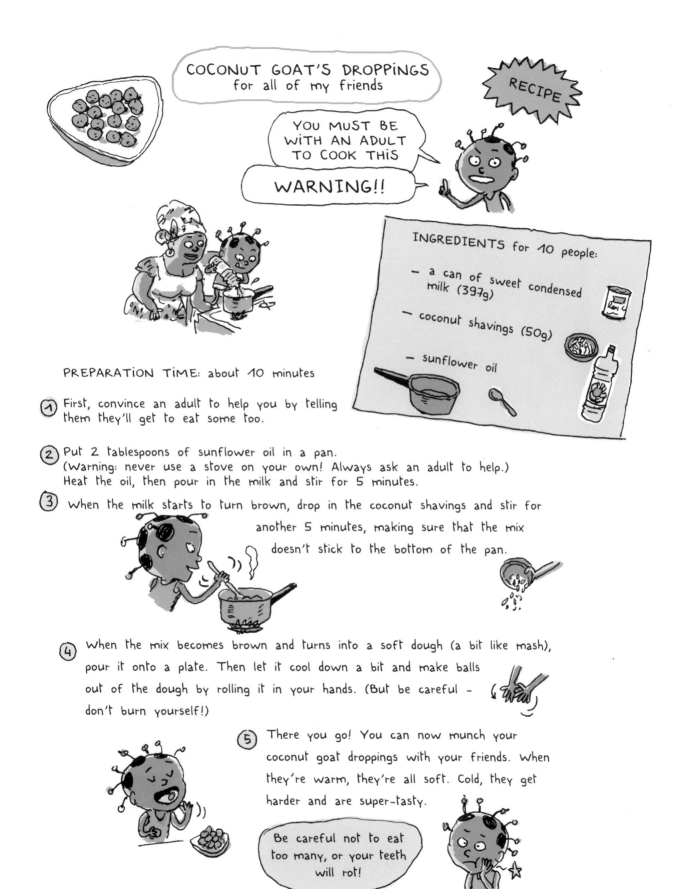

COMING SOON
FROM FLYING EYE BOOKS

FLYINGEYEBOOKS.COM

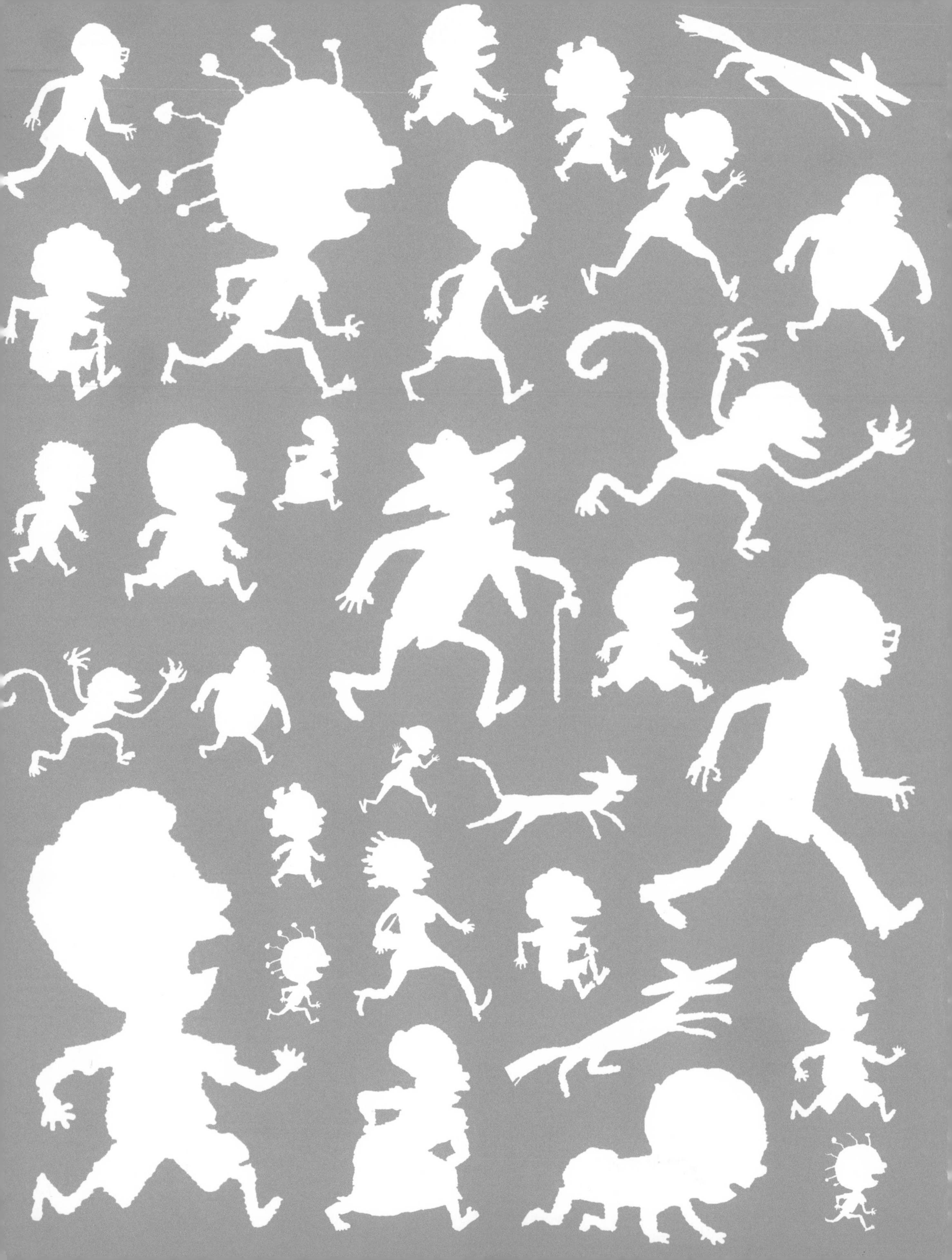